Books by Sally M. Russell:

An Escape For Joanna
*Finding A Path To Happiness
*Dr. Wilder's Only True Love
*Josh and the Mysterious Princess

*The Haven of Rest Ranch Series

D1714532

Josh

and the

Mysterious Princess

SALLY M. RUSSELL

authorHOUSE®

AuthorHouse™
1663 Liberty Drive
Bloomington, IN 47403
www.authorhouse.com
Phone: 1-800-839-8640

© 2011 Sally M. Russell. All rights reserved.

*No part of this book may be reproduced, stored
in a retrieval system, or transmitted by any means
without the written permission of the author.*

First published by AuthorHouse 6/24/2011

ISBN: 978-1-4634-1857-1 (e)
ISBN: 978-1-4634-1858-8 (sc)

Library of Congress Control Number: 2011910161

Printed in the United States of America

*Any people depicted in stock imagery provided by Thinkstock are models,
and such images are being used for illustrative purposes only.
Certain stock imagery © Thinkstock.*

This book is printed on acid-free paper.

*Because of the dynamic nature of the Internet, any web addresses or
links contained in this book may have changed since publication and
may no longer be valid. The views expressed in this work are solely those
of the author and do not necessarily reflect the views of the publisher,
and the publisher hereby disclaims any responsibility for them.*

This book is dedicated to all young lovers who put their faith in God and let Him open the doors for them. Life turns out so much better if God is there beside you.

"You're a hard one to find, Miss Becker, but I hope you're going to let me dance with you." Josh thought he had almost begged, but he'd quickly taken her hand and started toward the dance floor. He was so glad when she hadn't resisted.

> Let the heavens rejoice,
> let the earth be glad, let
> them say among the
> nations, "The Lord reigns!
> I Chronicles 16:31

Chapter One

October 15, 2005

It was a beautiful October afternoon and Josh Holcomb was standing straight and tall at the arbor waiting to watch the bridal attendants come down the red brick path. He'd arrived late yesterday afternoon from college so he could attend the rehearsal dinner hosted by his parents and then be the best man for his brother, Jon, who was marrying Christy Hayes in an outdoor ceremony at the Haven of Rest Ranch. Christy's brother, Brent, and cousin, Brad, had seated the guests and then joined the two brothers at the arbor.

The tall maple trees, in their vivid fall colors, formed a canopy of shade as well as beauty over the yard that had been decorated with huge containers of shrubs and lovely flowers. The arbor itself was covered with its natural vines, and beautiful live flowers had been inserted today to enhance the ethereal elegance.

It was now 3 o'clock and the first attendant exited the house and started toward the arbor where Jon and Christy would exchange their vows. Josh had known that Liz Becker, Christy's cousin, was to be one of the three attendants, but he was absolutely mesmerized as she strolled so demurely toward them. He knew she was only 16, but today, in her beautiful rust gown and carrying a bouquet of yellow spider mums and baby's breath, she could easily pass for a young fashion model.

Josh hadn't seen Liz since they'd met back in July, and there was sure a lot of that weekend that he'd like to forget. His brother had been hired by Noah Hayes, Christy's grandfather and owner of the Hayes Law Firm, back in April, and Christy worked there as a paralegal. Noah had invited Jon and his family to the 4th of July festivities held at the ranch, and Liz's family had driven down from Colorado Springs. Liz is the daughter of Christy's Aunt Rachel and Uncle David, who is a pediatrician with his practice in Colorado Springs.

Josh, for some uncontrollable reason, had started teasing Liz soon after they'd been introduced. Liz had endured it through lunch and a game of doubles in tennis on Saturday, but she'd finally had enough and had gone inside the house to avoid him. After he'd gone riding with Jon and Christy for awhile in the afternoon, he'd decided to try to find her and apologize.

In the nice cozy library of the main house, where Christy's parents and brother live, he'd found Liz curled up in a chair reading a Ranch and Farm magazine. "I'm sorry for upsetting you," he'd whispered but had also included a little kiss on the cheek. "I'd just been trying to get your attention because I was captivated by your sweet smile and those beautiful brown eyes. They're so unusual with your pretty blonde hair." When he'd only received a reprimand in return, he'd then informed her that dinner was almost ready.

He'd begun to think he may have carried the teasing a little too far and she wouldn't have anything more to do with him. He'd also been concerned that the difference in their ages might be bothering her. After all, he'd be a senior in college and she'd only be a sophomore in high school this fall. When she'd finally walked outside, he may have been just a little too forward again, but he'd been able to save her the embarrassment of grabbing a plate from the table before a prayer had been said. He'd quickly whispered for her to slap his face and then explained why as he picked her up and headed toward her parents. He'd hoped it would draw attention away from the table, and she'd certainly given him a wallop. Actually, it had been the second time that day, the first being on the tennis court, but this time she'd apologized and had even thanked him in front of her parents. Luckily, Sunday had passed without incident while attending church services and enjoying the festivities at the ranch.

Everything had started off well when the group of 18 decided to go horseback riding Monday afternoon, the 4th of July, too. To his surprise, Liz had agreed to ride beside him, and they were having a real good time until his horse had been spooked so suddenly he hadn't had a chance to react. He'd been thrown off, knocked unconscious, and rushed to the hospital in Colorado Springs. Dr. Becker had been on the ride and had immediately taken charge of the situation, but Josh had remained unconscious until after the lunch hour on Tuesday. He'd then almost magically awakened and found Liz sitting beside his bed.

The attending surgeon, Dr. Dan Wilder, who had set his broken arm and checked the x-rays that had been taken upon arrival for possible internal injuries, along with his bruised ribs and the lump on his head, had casually referred to Liz as a fairy-tale princess but had given no explanation why. Josh had called her his angel, but she wasn't revealing anything out of the ordinary. The nurse had come in just as he'd asked Liz if she'd kissed him to wake him up, so of course, she hadn't answered. Her dad and Jon had both come shortly after that, and she'd left with her dad after whispering in Josh's ear that she'd see him again before he was released. Josh had, however, continued to wonder why Dr. Wilder had called her a fairy-tale princess. Had he actually seen something happen but was leaving it up to Liz to tell him? The next morning, Wednesday, Josh had *really* been surprised when she'd actually walked in and stayed until he'd been released and Jon had come to pick him up that afternoon.

While the brothers had been visiting Tuesday evening, Jon had told Josh about the events of Monday afternoon. "Liz had run over to me and almost begged to ride with us to the hospital when it was decided that I'd drive the rest of the family in the ranch van. Our folks had ridden with you, along with Dr. Becker, and I'd driven the ranch van so there'd be plenty of room for everyone to return to the ranch. Jacob, Janice, Christy and Liz were all here for the wait to see if you were going to be all right. It had really been a great help that Liz was along because she knew where the hospital was without me having to stop and ask somewhere along the way. Christy may have known, but she hadn't said anything. We were all hoping, of course, that you would be riding back with us, but you'd apparently landed much harder than any of us had imagined.

Later, when we could visit your room, but only two at a time, Christy and I had asked Liz if she would like one of us to go in with her, but she, looking a little sheepish and embarrassed, asked if she could go in alone. She must have had something special to say to you," he'd chuckled.

"Maybe she *has* been my guardian angel. She certainly has been attentive, all of which I've relished," Josh had responded. But still, he had never quite been able to get their age difference off his mind.

Now, bringing his thoughts back to the wedding, Josh watched admiringly as Liz had almost reached the arbor, advanced to her place and then turned to watch the others as they came down the path and also took their places for the ceremony. Susan Ferris, the girlfriend of Christy's brother, Brent, stood next to Liz, and Mary, Liz's sister, was Maid of Honor. Christy had been absolutely glowing as she'd walked down the path, in a gorgeous gown, with her father. The twin siblings of Jon and Josh had then sung a duet, and later in the ceremony, they had each sung a solo.

It had been a beautiful wedding, from start to

finish, and now the reception was really cool set up in the big barn. Josh could hardly wait for the music to start because he wanted to take advantage of the chance to talk and dance with Liz. He felt they'd become pretty good friends by the time he'd left the hospital, so he was hoping she'd be willing to dance with him.

She'd been escorted by her brother during the recessional, but had somehow disappeared, so he'd been looking all over for her. He was just beginning to think she'd gone into the house again to avoid him, but when he turned to look toward the door of the barn, considering whether or not to go to the house, she was suddenly standing in front of him. "Hi, Josh," she whispered.

"You're a hard one to find, Miss Becker, but I hope you're going to let me dance with you." Josh thought he'd almost begged, but he'd quickly taken hold of her hand and started toward the dance floor. He was so glad when she hadn't resisted.

"I guess I can fit you in for at least one dance since you did such a nice job as best man for your brother," she smirked. When they were on the dance floor, though, and he'd bent down slightly to dance cheek to cheek during the first slow number, she'd quickly pushed away. It was a big disappointment to him, but he just rested his chin on the top of her head since she was so tiny. He soon realized that was making her rather tense also, so he straightened up and was relieved when that song was over. The next one was a much more relaxing dance for both of them because it was a fast number. Of course, he was elated when the one dance she'd promised turned into almost every single one.

"Would you like to get something to eat or drink?" Josh asked as the band took its first break. "The smell of all that food has suddenly made my stomach start to growl, and I'd better feed it before it has all the people in the barn wondering what the terrible noise is," he chuckled.

"I'd like that and it does sound like your stomach could use some nourishment," she giggled. "I think my mom was going to be serving the punch, but all kinds of things were prepared, so whenever you're ready, let's see about satisfying that stomach. I know there's shrimp, hot wings, little smokies, roast beef, potato salad and fruit salads on one table; and there's sandwich fixings, relishes and chips with two or three different dips, several yummy cheeses and a lot of fresh fruits on another. All the soft drinks and wine are available at the bar set up over there beside the dance floor."

"I'm ready whenever you are."

As they headed toward the food laden tables, Josh

remarked, "Since I'm still just a growing boy, all that food sounds great, but weren't some of us supposed to take Jon and Christy for a ride around the area? I thought, as best man, I was responsible for getting that little job done, but I'm not exactly sure when or how I'm supposed to do it. This is my first time at being a best man, or even to attend a big affair like this."

Nodding, Liz said, "Let's get some food first and then we'll see if we can get the two of them in Jon's car. It'll be fun if we can get some other cars to follow us and make a lot of noise honking the horns, flashing their lights, and some cans dangling on the back of Jon's car. I think Brent and Brad were planning to get the cans tied on, and they had also mentioned something about setting off some fireworks."

"It's probably not quite dark enough for fireworks yet, so I guess we can eat first and then find them and see what their plans are."

"I'll agree to that," she said as she took his hand and started toward the food tables.

A little later, they found Brent and Brad, and the newlyweds were just finishing a slow dance. They ushered them into Jon's Tahoe, that did have the cans tied to the back, and then Josh drove them around the town and even down to the lake for a good 20 or 25 minutes. Quite a few cars had followed with horns blasting and their lights flashing, but when they'd reached Main Street in town, they'd heard the police siren and thought they were going to be in trouble. It was actually one of the police officers who quickly got at the head of the procession and was the one who'd led them clear down to the lake.

True to their word, Brent and Brad had quite a fireworks display set up. Almost everyone came running out of the barn, when the first boom went off, because they didn't realize what was happening, but then they really enjoyed watching the sky light up.

When they returned to the reception, Aunt Rachel came quickly and led Christy and Jon away to a beautifully decorated table. It was time for the traditional cutting of the cake by the bride and groom.

"Oh, they're going to cut their cake now, Josh. Let's get closer," Liz said excitedly as she grabbed his hand and started pulling him to where the action was taking place. He'd been a little surprised, but definitely thrilled, when Liz had come to him after the wedding and acted as if she were his date and was really glad to see him. Maybe she thought she was still his guardian angel. They watched as the happy newlyweds fed each other some of the cake and also, with a cup of punch in their hands, they hooked their arms for a toast. They really appeared to be in a dream world all of their own.

Shortly after that was finished, the single girls were asked to gather around so that Christy could toss her bouquet. Most every girl involved was so excited because she'd had a dream of catching the bride's bouquet and being the next bride to walk down the aisle.

"I'm going to count to three, and then it's going to fly," Christy called. "One, two, and three," she shouted and the bouquet was soon flying high through the air like one of those big graceful birds. Closer and closer and closer it came toward the group of young ladies, all with their hands outstretched and their eyes fixed on the flowers coming their way. When it finally came down, no one could've been more surprised than Liz when it landed right in her arms. Since she's still so young, she had never given a thought to being the one who would catch the bride's bouquet. She certainly didn't have any plans for marriage, and she'd gotten in the group just for the fun of it. Some of the older girls seemed rather disappointed, and one, who had just gotten engaged, was so hoping for confirmation that she might be the next bride. They were all good sports, however, and came over to congratulate Liz before they walked away.

Josh had stood watching, but his mind had also been wandering to other things. He had always thought he was too busy having fun to take time to pray, to go to church, or to even read the Bible like the rest of his family. They'd tried to encourage and guide him, but he'd had his own ideas and plans for his life. After all, wasn't there something about God helping those who help themselves? He was sure he'd heard that somewhere.

Tonight, for some reason, his mind was playing tricks on him. He knew that Liz, Jon and Christy were all Christians, and they sure seemed to have something that he didn't. He'd seen it in Jon and Christy's eyes; a contentment that he's certainly missing. He'd never felt vibes before like the ones he was having around Liz today, either, especially when her big brown eyes had smiled at him or when he was holding her while on the dance floor.

She never seems the least bit unsettled or apprehensive like I do. But, shucks, I'm not ready for any commitment, personal or religious. I've got the rest of this year of college and then I have to learn all about managing the farm by working with Dad. That's going to take a lot of concentration so I don't have time right now for anything else. It's especially true about getting involved with a little sixteen-year-old. It must be just the fun of seeing her again; remembering the good times we had; plus I haven't even had a date since returning to school in late August. I must really be slipping, but I haven't been attracted to anyone until I saw Liz today at the wedding. What can this all mean anyway?

He suddenly recalled how he'd felt back in July when Jon was talking about giving Christy the engagement ring. He'd thought then that he really wouldn't mind if Liz was wearing his ring, and that was after knowing her for only four short days.

I can't believe that I could've even considered that. I must not have been thinking straight, or I hadn't fully recovered from the concussion. It's all so weird because it's Liz who is involved, a little sixteen-year-old. He was standing there with a deep frown on his face and hadn't even noticed that a very excited Liz was running toward him.

Her voice startled him. "Josh, can you believe it? I caught Christy's bouquet!" she'd exclaimed as she'd approached him. "I never ever thought that it would come right into my hands." She stopped short when she saw the expression on his face. "What's wrong, Josh? You look as if you're worried about something."

"No, I'm fine, Liz." he was quick to reply as he snapped back into the present. "I was just thinking about something that was a little disconcerting, that's all."

"Anything I can help you with?"

"No, Liz, just forget I said anything. It's something

I have to figure out on my own." Realizing he may have sounded a little harsh, he tried to change the subject. "I'm sorry, Liz, but it looks like Christy and Jon may have gone to change clothes, so I guess they'll be leaving soon. I'm sure going to miss my big brother now that he's married and probably won't have much time for his family anymore. We had always been pretty close while growing up, but I suppose it happens in all families sooner or later. I guess I wasn't expecting it to be so soon."

"You'll still be brothers, Josh. Just be thankful he's not clear across the country. With good roads and better cars these days, distances don't seem quite so bad. I know we drive down here to the ranch quite often to keep in touch with Mom's family. Would you like to get a little more to eat and dance at least once more before the band decides to stop playing?" she smiled as she patted his cheek.

"I'm right with you, Liz, but I want to hold you a little closer this time if it's a slow dance number. Are you going to let me do that?"

"I'll think about it, but your cheek is much too high for me to reach in these low, no-heel slippers I'm wearing. Maybe I could just stand on your toes while you move around the dance floor." she giggled.

"If that's the only way I can dance cheek to cheek with you, we just might try that little maneuver. By the way, does that distance remark you made about Jon refer to you and me getting together again in the future, too?"

"It could, I guess, if my family happens to be at the ranch when you come to visit."

"In other words, you're not going to let me come to Colorado Springs and take you out on a date?"

"My folks have a rule that I can't date, like a single couple, until I'm eighteen. My dad feels college is soon enough for girls to spread their wings. If it were sort of a double date, like with Christy and Jon last summer, then I suppose we could possibly consider our time together a date. I wonder, now that you mentioned a date, if Mom or Dad did whisper anything to Christy when we were going to be with her and Jon," she giggled.

"O.K, Miss Becker, you and your parents win. There'll be no actual dates and we'll just be good buddies tagging along with Christy and Jon when we're at the ranch. Come on, let's dance. I can at least hold you while we're dancing."

Jon and Christy had gone, but the band played for the dancers and eaters for another hour or more. Josh and Liz danced some more, ate some more, and talked some more until the music stopped. It had certainly been a great day, and everything had gone so well.

Josh walked slowly to the house with Liz while

15

trying to act unaffected with the thought that they probably wouldn't be seeing each other again for who knows how long. He finally said, "Well, I imagine college is going to keep me pretty busy the rest of this year, and I'm sure you'll have a lot of activities at school, too, but maybe we could try to exchange a note now and then. Would you possibly have e-mail available?"

"I'd love to keep in touch by e-mail, Josh, but I'm surprised that you'd even want to keep in touch with me. You probably have a lot of pretty girls to date at college. I missed seeing you at the Fall Festival in September, but Jon said the professors were loading you down with a lot of work already. The distance was a factor, too, he said, because your arm still bothered you when you were driving. Keeping in touch by e-mail will help, but I sure hope I get to see you before next summer. That seems like such a long time without being able to give each other a hard time," she giggled.

"Gosh, Liz, you're making me lonesome already. Maybe we should try sharing one of those magical kisses, like in fairy tales, before we have to say goodbye. Wouldn't it be great to experience something magical together like I did in the hospital? I suppose my folks are beginning to wonder where I am, but they may have gone on without me since I have my own car. Jacob and I are staying at Jon's apartment tonight and then we'll drive down home tomorrow. It's back to school for me on Monday where I'll have a few classes to make up."

It was silent for just a minute and then he started singing, "Give me a little kiss, will you, Liz? Just one little kiss, will you, Liz?"

He was really caught by surprise when she suddenly stood on the top of his shoe and then up on tiptoe to kiss him on the lips very quickly but tenderly. Even then, it was almost all she could do to reach his lips because Josh wasn't bending down. He hadn't even known what she was up to or there most likely would've been a little more to that kiss. He just stood there looking at her as she timidly backed away.

"It may have been a little short, but I certainly enjoyed it, Liz. However, that one was from you to me, but this one is going to be from me to you," he whispered as he then pulled her into his arms, held her rather closely, and kissed his little angel with feelings he had never felt before. His head was spinning and he felt as if he'd landed on a beautiful isle of paradise. Trying so hard to stay in control, he swallowed and then asked, "Are you ever going to tell me if you were the one who woke me up with that fabulous kiss in my room at the hospital?"

"Maybe, some day," she smiled, "although it's a lot

of fun keeping you guessing for a change since you're always teasing or pulling some trick," she giggled.

"I'm sorry I teased you so much that first day, Liz. I'll try to be a good boy."

"Well, I suppose we'd better part now, Josh. I do hope you're having a great year at college, and I'll pray that God will always keep you safe. Maybe you'll remember the verse that promises that wherever you are, God will be with you." As she turned and hurried into the house, Josh had noticed the tears welling up in her eyes.

He was a bit choked up himself as he stood and watched until the door had closed behind her and she was gone. As he slowly walked toward his car, he was trying to figure out what had actually happened to him today and why he was feeling so strange. *Has a mere sixteen-year-old been able to break down my resistance to falling in love?* "No way," he muttered as he climbed into his Tahoe, "but now she has me talking to myself? It can't be. It's just the sentimentality of the wedding, seeing my big brother married and so happy, and also getting to hold that sweet little sixteen-year-old girl in my arms to dance with and give a goodbye kiss to. I'll be all right tomorrow."

Chapter Two

Josh was trying to study, but his mind kept wandering back to the wedding and how much he had enjoyed being with Liz. Even though he struggled to concentrate, he just kept remembering the fun he'd had at the wedding. *I wonder what she's doing or thinking right now. Could she be thinking about me, too? Oh, I just have too much time on my hands since I gave up the football practices.*

When Josh had decided he wouldn't play football when he entered college because of his study load, the coach had asked if he would at least help him at practices. Since it was his former high school coach who had become the coach at this college, the same year Josh had become a freshman, he had agreed to work with the football team just during practices, and his hours had been filled his first three years. He'd really enjoyed that, but after the fall off the horse in July resulting with a concussion, a broken arm and the bruised ribs, he'd decided to take his senior year a little easier and maybe study a bit harder.

However, after two and a half months, he's become restless and he feels like he needs something to do besides study. His thoughts began wandering. *I'd like someone to talk to, but why do I keep thinking about Liz so much? For heaven's sake, she's only sixteen years old, but it's amazing how she shows more maturity than most girls I've met in either high school or college.* He was soon picturing her again in his mind--her long silky blonde hair and those unusual brown eyes which seemed to search deep into a person's soul. He'd noticed that her dad also had the brown eyes with his dark hair, Brad had the dark hair but blue eyes, and her mother and Mary both had blonde hair and blue eyes like the rest of the Hayes family. Liz was the only one of her family who'd gotten the extraordinary brown eyes and blonde hair combination, and it was really striking.

She'd also loved all of his hobbies--riding, playing tennis, and swimming, but he'd really been surprised when she was even interested in the operation of the ranch, which he thought surprising for a girl who had been raised in the city. She'd told him once that she'd love to live there all the time instead of in Colorado Springs. That had made him wonder if she could love his family's farm as much as she loved The Haven of Rest ranch. "Oh, come on now, where did that come from?" he muttered as he slammed his book closed.

He shoved his chair back from the desk and stood up. He paced in the small space of his room for a couple minutes, then grabbed his coat and headed out the door. He'd thought a walk might help so he strolled aimlessly down the street until he found himself outside the door of a little cafe he knew was a college hangout.

Maybe I'll get a coke before going back to my room, he mused, but just after he'd stepped inside, he heard his name being called. Glancing toward a large corner booth, he saw several members of the football team.

"Hey, come and join us, Josh. We'll buy you a drink."

He ordered a coke and carried it to the booth. He was a little shocked to see so many empty beer bottles scattered around the table, plus the ones they were holding in their hands. "Aren't you guys supposed to be in training?" he asked.

"Oh, what the coaches don't know won't hurt them," one big 280# defensive lineman said and then let out a big laugh. "We're just relaxing a little, Josh, but we'll be ready to play Saturday. Let us buy *you* a beer. You're 21 and legal."

"I don't think so tonight, Jake, but let me remind you that your coach is pretty good at sensing a change in reflexes, attitude and abilities that those drinks likely will alter from your normal skills. There was once in high school that three of the guys on the team had a couple of beers thinking they would be fine at practice the next day. The only thing they got at practice, however, was a two-game suspension. Luckily they learned their lesson and all went well for the rest of the season. I need to get back to my room pretty soon and do a little more studying, so this coke will suffice. I'm not too much into beer drinking anyway."

He'd then noticed, most surprisingly, that most of the guys had slowly pushed their bottles away and had turned their full attention on him. "Why aren't you working with us this year, Josh? You're not getting soft in your senior year, are you?" the big Center asked, and the whole group erupted in laughter. "Seriously, we really learned a lot from you and we miss having you out on the field during practice."

"Thanks, but I just couldn't bear the thought of poor little me up against all you big hunks for another football season," he chuckled. "Actually, I was afraid of another broken arm, or a concussion, or some more bruised ribs. One set of those was enough for me this year without facing you guys on the field." He'd taken a drink of his coke and leaned back just to listen to their conversation, but they seemed more interested in him.

"Tell us what happened to you, Josh. We'd heard that the horse you were riding got spooked and threw you. With your riding ability, you must have really been distracted by something, or someone, to let a horse do that to you. Did you have a cute little filly riding beside you?" All of them laughed at the question, but then waited anxiously for his reply.

"You know, I hadn't given much thought to that before. I was riding a strange horse on a completely new trail when something jumped over in the tall grasses, my horse reared and I was thrown off. It all happened so quickly that I didn't have time to react. But, to answer your question about my riding companion, she was something else--the cutest little sixteen-year-old, smart as they come, and she only had eyes for me." Chuckling, he added,

"I only wish."

"Oh, oh, she got to you, huh?"

"I only wish she were a little older so I could see where it could go."

"Temptation can be a downfall, Josh, and you know you can't have any fun with a sixteen-year-old or you might end up in prison for life. You'd better let us fix you up with one that is hot and ready."

"No thanks, Guys. That isn't what I'm looking for. I want someone I can love and cherish for a lifetime. I guess going to my brother's wedding last month and seeing their devotion to one another got to me more than I realized," he chuckled. He had finished his coke, and as he slipped from the booth, he added, "And with that little gem of wisdom, I'll take my leave and go study for an exam tomorrow. See you around, and you'd better play well Saturday. I'll be watching." As he started toward the door, he realized that the booth was emptying. *Were they actually taking my remarks about the coach seriously? I really hope so because I'd hate to see any of them get into trouble.*

"Come and see us when you get tired of waiting for your little cutie to grow up," one of them remarked, and he could hear their laughter fill the room. However, his mind started whirling as he thought about what they had said. *Can I actually wait for over two years for Liz to grow up? I wonder when her next birthday is because sophomores are not usually 17. Has she been stretching the truth about her age? She definitely did mention at the wedding that she'd be 17 before too long, but I think I'll check with Jon and Christy. I want to know for sure, and for some reason, I don't want to miss her next birthday. She kissed me at the wedding, and I **think** I got to kiss her while she's still sweet 16, but I do wonder if she kissed me that day* *in the hospital. I am sure something woke me from that unconscious state I was in, but I guess I'm not going to find out from her. Maybe, if I can play my cards right, I'll get to be the first one to give her a kiss after her 17th birthday. All I can say is, she'd better be turning 17.*

"Hey, Josh, is your mind still on that little filly? You're almost past your dorm."

The remark and laughing from the guys driving by snapped him back to reality, and he was just a little embarrassed when he saw that they were right. He then decided to just keep walking when he realized the library would still be open for a few more minutes. Maybe he could find a book and get started on researching a paper he has to write.

Josh got some good studying done, when he got back to his room, and even read a few pages of the book he'd found. He actually aced his Business exam the next morning, and then spent two hours in the library, during the afternoon, doing quite a bit more research on his paper about 'types of soil and their uses' for Agriculture Studies.

He stopped on his way to the dorm and bought a pizza and a big Gatorade because he didn't want to go to the cafeteria. He wanted to work on this paper for awhile and then he'd call Jon and Christy.

Why am I so anxious to find out when Liz's

birthday is and her exact age anyway? I just have this gut feeling that I might miss it if I don't ask pretty soon, but why would it matter? Of course, it could be that I'm hoping it's real soon so she'll turn eighteen that much sooner. I just can't understand these feelings toward Liz when she's actually too young for me to even consider dating. She told me that she can't even date, without a chaperone, until she's eighteen, or is that another little stretch of the truth? What a puzzle life can be, but we've had a lot of fun together, and a chaperone wasn't a problem with Jon and Christy along with us. Come to think of it, I never heard any comment from her parents about having a chaperone. Do you suppose that little smarty said that just to keep me at a distance? He had to laugh as he was thinking he may have been outsmarted by that little rascal.

Jon and Christy have been living in her apartment, since coming home from their honeymoon, although some of Jon's things are still in the other one, like his treadmill and a lot of his clothes because of lack of closet space. They're already talking about building a house out on the ranch. Josh dialed their number, but there was no answer. "They're most likely taking their walk. I'll call them later," he mumbled as he clicked off.

He then sat looking at the phone for only a few seconds before picking it up and automatically pushing the numbers to call Liz. *Why am I doing this?* He was definitely questioning this action when he heard her answer.

"Hello, Becker residence, Liz speaking."

"Hey, Liz, it's Josh. I just wanted to tell you that I aced one exam today and got a lot of research done for my paper in Ag. What have you been up to?"

"Josh, it's good to hear from you. I'm proud of you for acing your test. My day has been the same old thing. Spanish, French and English are the only subjects I really like, but I know Math and History are important, too. One thing is really exciting, though. My Spanish teacher has been talking about a trip to Spain during Spring break and taking a few of us with her. Doesn't that sound neat? The only downer is that she'll require us to speak Spanish all the time we're there. I just don't know if I'm that good."

"You can do it, Liz. It just takes a little extra concentration on your part, but how old do they require a student to be before they can travel like that?"

"I don't know, but it wouldn't be a problem for me. I'll be seventeen before Spring break. Our family took a trip to England and Scotland a couple of years ago so I already have my passport." There was a slight pause and then he heard a giggle. "Josh Holcomb, was that a sneaky way just to find out when I'm going to have my birthday?"

"Liz Becker, how can you read my mind, even over the phone? But, yeah, I do want to know when your birthday will be so I can be there to give you your first real grown up kiss after you turn another year older. I should be sorry I spoiled your 'sweet sixteen and never been kissed' status, but I'm not because you kissed me first--maybe even twice, if you'd only admit it. Oops, your parents aren't listening, are they?" he chuckled. "Sooo, are you going to tell me or do I have to find out from Christy?"

"I'll tell you when my birthday is if you'll tell me when you're going to be 22."

"How do you know I'll be 22? I may be turning 21, like Brad."

"That information was out a long time ago, Josh. Your brother came to our spring barbecue at the ranch, and I overheard Brad and him talking about their siblings' ages. I am sure you found out about me being sixteen from that conversation, too."

Well, I guess her being 16 is correct. "Okay, tell me when you'll be 17 and then I'll tell you when I'll be 22."

"This could go back and forth all night, you know, so I'll just tell you that mine is February 14th.

I was my parents' Valentine that year. Now, when's yours?"

"Is that really the truth, Liz, or are you trying to keep something from me again?"

"That's the truth, Josh. What do you think I've been keeping from you?"

"Oh, it's nothing really unless you were spoofing me about the chaperone rule."

"The chaperone requirement is usually enforced. I don't know how you rated at the ranch except that they probably assumed Christy and Jon wouldn't let us be alone, and if I know my parents, Dad or Mom probably whispered in their ear. They're pretty good at getting what they want in a roundabout way. But, come on, Josh, it's your turn to tell me when your birthday will be."

"So you were a cuddly little Valentine, huh? I'm sort of surprised they didn't give you a name like Candy, or Valerie, or Evangeline, or maybe Valentina," he chuckled.

"Josh, you're being an unbearable tease again. Now, tell me when you were born or I'm not speaking to you ever again!"

"I'm going to tell you, but you probably won't believe me. I was an April fool to *my* parents. I really was born on April 1st, on the great April Fool's Day."

"I know another person who was born on April

1st, and he's the most intelligent, the warmest and most friendly man I have ever met. Would you like to know who he is?"

"I certainly would. I need all the encouragement I can get."

"It's my Grandpa Noah. Now, do you still feel so April Foolish?" she giggled.

"Well, Sweet Valentine, you always make my day. It's nice to know that such a great man like Mr. Hayes and I share the same birthday. Maybe as I get to know him, I'll be able to copy some of his good traits. But, don't you like the great combination we make, a pretty little Valentine and an April fool?"

"I could probably think of some nicer combinations, but I don't think ours is that odd or unusual and definitely not disgusting."

"Well, I'm glad you're not turned off by it. For now, though, I suppose I'd better let you go. I hope you didn't have anything else urgent to get done tonight. I've actually got another test tomorrow so I'd better study a bit more. Until we meet or talk again, I hope all your dreams will be happy ones, with me in them, of course, and you'll feel my warm lips against yours as you fall asleep." Chuckling, he just whispered, "Goodnight, Princess."

"You paint a pretty picture, Josh, but I may just wait until I see you in person. I'm not too crazy about

substitutes, especially since I've tasted the real thing."
He could hear her giggling and then a soft and so
sweet "Goodnight, Josh."

"Whoa, don't you hang up yet, Miss Becker. Are
you telling me that you really did enjoy the kisses
we've shared? That is the sweetest thing you've ever
said to me, Liz, and I have goose bumps just thinking
about it. I'm looking forward to seeing if we can
improve on them the next time we're together. Of
course, I still want to know if you kissed me in my
hospital room, too."

"Don't get your hopes up, Mr. Senior in College,
because I may meet someone who has a much sweeter
kiss than yours before I see you again."

"It may be sweeter, but it couldn't have any more
feeling in it than the one I gave you after the wedding
reception. I haven't forgotten the one you gave me
either. It does make me wonder, though, what your
parents would do if they found out about our kisses
since you keep telling me that you're not supposed to
be kissed until you're seventeen."

"I'm not going to tell them. Yours was one that I
think would be hard to beat, but since you are so far
away, I may need to test a few others to see how they
compare with yours. Goodnight, Josh."

"Goodnight, you little devil, but remember you'll
always be My Sweet Mysterious Princess, and some

day I'm going to learn the truth about that kiss in my hospital room."

"I'm so glad about the first and we'll see about the second," he heard her whisper just before she cradled the phone.

He couldn't think of studying, so he lay on his bed and thought of all the things he and Liz had done in the few times they had been together before and after his accident. Jon and Christy had been very good chaperones, and he felt that he and Liz had formed a pretty good friendship. The only problem is that he'd been feeling like he wanted a little more than just friendship since they were together last month at the wedding. *Could it really be possible that the two of us could someday be as close as Jon and Christy seem to be? I still can't understand where all this is coming from. She is absolutely too young and I need to get that through this thick skull of mine. But, why is she so often in my thoughts?*

He finally fell asleep with her still on his mind and a pillow in his arms that he was holding as close as he wished he were holding Liz. They were such sweet dreams.

Chapter Three

Finished with his pre-holiday exams, Josh was almost ready to head home for the long break between Thanksgiving and New Years. He was anxious to get on Moonlight, and ride out over the fields with the wind in his face and nothing to be concerned about for almost six weeks. The term seemed to have gone pretty fast, with Jon's wedding and then that sweet little Liz to talk to on the phone and e-mail occasionally. *It's amazing how she's become so important to me. Am I thinking of her just as a little sister, someone I want to care for and protect, or are all of these feelings going to put me into a situation I don't think I'm ready for? Oh, brother, what have I gotten myself into?*

She probably isn't home from school yet, but I'll leave an e-mail for her anyway so she'll know I'm going to be home. See, I just can't help myself--I'm thinking about her way too often. He couldn't hold back a rumbling moan.

"Hi, Pipsqueak, just thought I'd let you know that I finished my exams this morning and will be heading home shortly. I'll call you from there. My Spanish exam wasn't so bad since you've been helping me via e-mail. I'd rather it had been side by side so I could've thanked you with a little hug, but that time will come. I'm looking forward to riding Moonlight, but wish you could be riding beside me. I'd love to be singing a good old Western song for you as we're trotting along. I know I don't have Jacob or Jon's singing voice, but I can carry a tune. Say Hi to your family for me and I'll talk to you soon."
Not Mr. Holcomb, just Josh.

That reminds him again, of course, that he'd been teasing her about calling him Mr. Holcomb since the day they'd met. She'd gotten so upset with him that she'd gone in the house and stayed almost all afternoon. When he'd found her and wanted to apologize, he'd impulsively kissed her on the cheek and she'd called him Mr. Holcomb when she'd reprimanded him for it. He'd told her that his father was Mr. Holcomb, he was just Josh.

Now, being on his way, he knew his foot was a little too heavy on the gas pedal because he was anxious to get home, but then he saw flashing lights a short distance ahead. He slowed down immediately, and as he approached the scene, he realized there had been what appeared to be a one-car accident. He pulled over to the side of the road and jumped out to see if there was anything he could do to help. There was only the one State Trooper at the scene, and he was trying to check the occupants who were still inside the small four-door compact car. Josh could see that it was up against the guardrail with the hood and grill crumpled like an accordion. Both front doors were still accessible, but he had noticed that the back door on the passenger side was standing ajar as if it had popped open from the force of the impact.

He approached the trooper who informed him that he had called for back up and for emergency vehicles, and he had determined that there were only the two occupants. They'd need to be checked and kept calm until the medics arrived, but just then steam had started spewing from the crushed radiator and they had to back away to keep from getting burned. They could hear moaning from inside the car so the two of them again slowly and carefully inched toward the car doors.

Josh started around to the other side of the car

and immediately caught sight of a child's car seat lodged between the car and the guard rail. His whole body was feeling numb and his stomach was doing flip flops as he raced to see the condition of the child. When he found that there was no child, he relaxed somewhat as he went to the front door to see about the other occupant. There was just enough room for him to force open the door and hear a young woman moaning and crying, "The Baby, The Baby!"

Josh again felt sick to his stomach, but by that time, another car had stopped to help. He was an off duty EMT so Josh asked if he could check the young woman and he would see about the car seat. He had checked under the car earlier so now he held his head for a second to think what he should do. He knew there was only one place left to look so he went to the end of the guard rail and started down the side of the ravine. He carefully kept his eyes searching for any movements while listening for any sound as he slowly advanced through the tall and thick growth of grasses and weeds. He was so afraid of what he would most likely find, but he knew he had to keep going.

He'd heard the ambulance and more cruisers arrive so he wanted to make sure the child was found, if there'd definitely been one, so he kept on watching and listening as he fought his way through even thicker growth. He'd gone another eight or ten yards before he'd seen it, a small patch of blue about 15 feet away from him. He moved as quickly as he could until he was beside the motionless blue bundle which had never touched the ground because the tall thick grasses had absorbed the shock of the fall. It proved to be a heavy snowsuit with a hood fastened over the head of a very small child. Its eyes were closed and he knew he shouldn't move it, in case of an injury. He screamed, "I need help down here. There's a small child!"

The EMT was immediately on his way down to where Josh and the child were since the ambulance personnel were now in charge at the accident scene. He tried to find a pulse in the wrist first but wasn't successful. He then opened the snowsuit at the top and did find a pulse in the neck. "The child's alive," he called, as Josh had already started to scramble back up the bank to make sure the Emergency Crew didn't take off with the mother and the father, not realizing there was also a baby.

Miraculously, the baby had survived being thrown from the car seat and landing in the biggest patch of tall, thick and heavy grasses Josh had ever seen. It was most likely in shock, but everyone was amazed but so thankful that Josh had heard the mother and had followed his instincts that the baby might've been thrown clear of the guardrail. The tow truck was there to remove the car and the ambulance was now on its way to the hospital.

Josh was again on his way home, but with a deeper respect for the speed limit and the hazards of driving. He was so relieved, however, when he turned into the driveway at the farm and knew he'd reached home safely. When he had parked his Tahoe near the barn where their few horses are kept, he just bowed his head and prayed, "God, my Protector and my Savior, I know I haven't taken the time to talk to You for quite a while, but after the experience I had today, I have to thank You for being there with me, and also with all the emergency crew, the accident victims, and especially for keeping the little baby safe.

I think I learned a valuable lesson today, and I want to know that You will always be there for me. I have been a rebel, of sorts, and thought I could do my own thing, but I now know that You didn't leave me, but I left You. Will You take me back and let me be your child? I know I'm not worthy, but I understand that You are a forgiving God, and I really need to be forgiven. Thank You, again, for this day, for my eyes being opened, and for my safe journey home. Amen."

He raised his head and realized that his mother was standing beside the car so he rolled down the window. "Are you all right?" she asked. "We heard

about an accident on the highway and were worried
that you might have been involved in some way since
you're later than you had thought you'd be."

All he could do was nod. It took a few seconds,
which seemed like hours, before he finally found his
voice. He then told his mother about the accident and
about finding the baby, which now caused him to
break down and cry. His mother had opened the truck
door and somehow managed to put her arms around
him and hold him until he could calm down. His dad
came out of the barn and hurriedly approached them.
"Is everything okay here?" he asked. Frances nodded
as she told him that Josh had been at the scene of the
accident that they had heard about on the radio, and
he was the one who had found the baby.

"What a frightening experience that must've
been, but we heard that the baby was safe," his dad
remarked.

"Thank God, and I'm all right now, too," Josh
sighed. "It just got to me, while I was telling Mom
what I'd seen today. I've suddenly realized just how
vulnerable we all are, and how God can save the most
unlikely without a scratch. Are you guys all right?"

"We're fine," his dad replied as he gave Frances
a look that silently asked if she'd heard that remark
from their rebel son. Turning back to Josh, he asked,
"Can we help you carry anything into the house? It's

good to see you home again even though it's only been a little over five weeks since the wedding in October. When do you go back?"

"I'm afraid you have me under foot for about six weeks. Classes start the 5th of January, but I'm planning to go back early and add a class to my schedule. Have you heard whether Jon and Christy will be coming down here for either of the holidays yet?"

"We've been invited to come for Thanksgiving at the ranch," his dad explained, "and then they would come down here the day after Christmas and stay part of that week with us. Matthew has been doing so well since he hired on in late June, I'm sure he can handle the chores along with the other two hired hands, so we'll just fly up and back on Thursday. Janice, of course, wants to stay here and cook Thanksgiving dinner for Matt. They're getting to be quite a twosome," he chuckled as they each took some of his things and headed for the house.

"At this time of year, had you given any thought to the possibility of maybe flying in a snowstorm, Dad? As much as I'd love to see the ranch, I understand they can have some rather big snows in Colorado this time of year."

"Well, your mother and I discussed the situation, have watched the weather reports for several days, and the forecasts look fairly good. It is a wonderful invitation, and that family your brother married into is really super."

"I'll second that remark," Josh chuckled. Of course, when they'd reached the big homey kitchen, he could smell the freshly baked cookies still cooling on the racks. He quickly grabbed a few, picked up his luggage, and headed for his room with the loving remark, "Thanks, Mom, for being such a wonderful mother."

Later that evening, he saddled Moonlight for a relaxing ride under the bright full moon and a sky full of twinkling stars. As he rode along, he found himself putting words to a little tune:

I am always wishing you were right here by my side
And how I'd love to have you along on this ride;
O'er the fields we would gallop,
Through the streams we would forge
But then we'd stop riding so we could, of course,
Share a kiss or two and I'd no longer be blue,
It'd prove that my Princess is really in love,
And that I'll always be in love with her, too.

What is it about you, Liz, that has my heart pounding every time I think of you. It's much too often for my own good, I'm afraid. I'll try to figure it out when we see each other Thursday and then I can put you out of my mind and be my old carefree self again.

Chapter Four

Flying to the ranch for Thanksgiving, however, turned into quite an experience. There had only been a light mist falling when they'd left the farm, but just now a rather dangerous snowstorm warning was being transmitted to Tom's radio suggesting that he land at the nearest airfield. He was alone in the cockpit, which he actually prefers, and he was trying to determine about how far they were still out from the ranch. He'd decided to just keep flying since there were no commercial airfields in the area, and he had actually calculated it to be about 25 minutes before they reached their destination. He felt he had a pretty good idea where he was and the direction of the ranch, and he certainly didn't want to worry the rest of the family, especially Frances.

It wasn't long, however, until the snow was getting so heavy that the visibility was minimal, but he was hoping he still might fly out of the storm since it had been reported to be scattered. He kept his eyes open for any break in the clouds and frequently checked his watch for the projected arrival time. The 25 minutes had seemed like hours and then, all of a sudden, the snowfall let up a little. As he studied the landscape, he was sure he'd seen several lights flashing a short distance ahead. *Could someone possibly be out on the field trying to signal us in? Of course, Jon was planning to pick us up at 10 o'clock, but would the Tahoe's lights flash that clearly?*

He decided he'd better ask Joshua if he'd please come forward. "What can you make out with those flashing lights down there, Son? We should be close to the ranch, but I can't determine for sure if that is it or what those lights are. Do you remember the lay of the land from the other trip?"

"Good Lord, Dad, why didn't you let me know what you were facing?"

"I was pretty sure where I was and of the time that would be required to get here."

Josh became very quiet as he studied the situation for a minute, and then he softly whispered, "Dad, there's a break in the clouds at 2 o'clock and I can see the outline of a truck. Yes, I'm pretty sure that's the ranch truck with the bar of lights flashing across the top of the cab. And, there are some more lights, maybe two and two, which could be the van and Jon's Tahoe flashing over to the left. It looks to me like they've tried to put lights on both sides of the airstrip so you need to land right between the two sets of lights."

"That's right on target with the direction I came in on for the 4th of July weekend, so let's say a prayer, Joshua, and ask for a safe landing. Dear Father, our constant Guide and Protector, we ask for your help right now to bring this plane in safely. We are in your hands and we believe in your divine love, power, and mercy. Amen."

"Amen," Josh added.

The landing was a little tricky with the snow having accumulated so quickly, but Tom was able, to his surprise, to set it down right in the middle of the runway. The wheels had skidded slightly, when they'd hit the snow, but then they had grabbed traction and held. He let out a big sigh as he cut the engines. "That was a little scarier than I would've liked," he very softly confessed, but he was still able to chuckle.

"You shouldn't have tried to do that all alone, Dad. Another set of eyes might've relieved some of the tension you must've been feeling."

"I'm sorry, Joshua, but I didn't want to worry

your mother, and if I had called for you any sooner it might have made her panic. We're safely on the ground now so let's not discuss it any more, OK?" he whispered.

"You're right, Dad. Let's see who's out here waiting for us, shall we?"

Jon was at the door of the plane when it opened and his expression gave away his worry and concern. As he gave them each a hug, he rasped, "I've never been so scared in my life. I knew you had most likely taken off when we heard the warning on TV, and I had no idea what to do. Noah was the one who suggested that we bring the truck with the bar of lights to mark the one side of the strip while the Tahoe and the big van, with their hazard lights, would give some flashing to catch your attention. For a while, the snowfall was so thick I didn't know if you'd be able to see the lights at all, and then, when I finally heard the plane, it sounded as if you'd gone right on past the ranch."

"Joshua recognized the truck with its lights flashing, and then he saw the other lights before I did. He realized you'd been marking the runway and directed me to land between them. We did circle so I could come in correctly, and the snow letting up a little didn't hurt a bit. I couldn't see anything for about 10 minutes up there, but Joshua's sharp eyes and God's guidance brought us in safely. Were you here all by yourself?"

"Brent and Joseph helped me get the van and trucks out here, Christy brought two of the horses out so they could get back to the house, and yes, I was here alone shaking in my boots most of the time. Two of the hired hands rode out and kept the snow cleared off as best they could, and two of you can help me drive the vehicles back."

"That's why I was able to get some traction then," Tom remarked. "I think I've had enough driving for awhile, though, so I'll let Jacob take my place behind the wheel, if that's all right with you."

"That's fine. Hey, Mom, are you going to come out of that plane?"

"I'm just getting my things together. That was quite a flight although your father didn't say a word until he finally called Joshua up to help him look for signs. I did get a little worried then. Of course, he hadn't told us about the storm warning--you know your father. Is there a lot of snow on the ground?"

"The guys don't think it'll last long because the sun is supposed to come through and warm everything up. You're here safe and sound, so let's get you to the house where it's warm and cozy and a lot of food to devour."

"I feel bad that I can't help with the meal. I did

bring some banana nut bread and some cranberry bread, but it seems like so little."

"It sounds good to me. You know how much I love those loaves of fruit bread that you make. They'll probably let you help in the kitchen, too, if you'd like." Looking into the plane, he asked, "Did you really let Janice stay home and cook for Matt?"

"Well, sort of. She also has to cook for Grandma and Grandpa Holcomb who are coming around noon. Of course, knowing Grandma, they'll be there a lot sooner than that because she doesn't think Janice is old enough to be out of diapers yet." Laughing, she continued, "Janice and I worked yesterday and got the turkey all ready to put in the oven, baked the pies, and fixed the sweet potato casserole so it's ready for the oven, too. Gran will help her with the stuffing, potatoes and gravy and any other details. She was putting the turkey in the oven when we were leaving. We even set the table yesterday, and she was planning to eat around two."

"You and Dad still think you're pretty clever when it comes to controlling your kids, don't you? I could never get away with anything when I was a teenager."

"Just remember where to come for advice when you need it, dear," she laughed.

The three vehicles took off slowly in the

approximately 3" of snow. It had almost stopped falling now, and they were soon in the warmth of the ranch house where the roaring fireplace was an inviting sight to the travelers. The four Holcomb men joined the other five men, plus Mary and Liz, who were all watching the Macy's Thanksgiving Day Parade. The Becker family had been lucky as they'd driven down from Colorado Springs yesterday before the weather had changed.

Mary and Liz had been excused from the kitchen detail to let the married women do their thing. It is one of the holidays when they let the hired kitchen staff have the day off to be with their own families, and the women love working together.

The aroma from the kitchen was breath taking, and Frances joined the other ladies to see if she could help in any way. They put her to work helping Christy finish washing and peeling the potatoes so they could start cooking. Rachel was working on the cranberry salad, and Marge was getting the sweet potatoes ready for the oven. Eleanor was making the dinner rolls at her house because she was positive her bread and rolls always turned out better in her own oven. Noah, as usual, was keeping her company. They arrived about 1 o'clock to join the festivities.

Everyone had been munching on relishes, crackers and cheese, and a nice warm cranberry drink while watching TV, but everything was ready at 1:45 and it looked like a gala banquet had been prepared.

When the meal was announced, they were all making their way toward the dining room when Liz moved over and grabbed Josh's hand so she could whisper to him. "I've got to talk to you before you leave today. I have a favor to ask."

"OK, that's great; I was hoping we could have some time alone. When and where do you suggest?"

"Josh and Liz, we're waiting patiently for you to join us so we can thank God for this delicious smelling food and eat. We're all starved," Joseph laughingly teased them.

"Sorry," they said simultaneously and took their places at the table. Then they all joined hands as Joseph led them in prayer.

It looked so very special with the 6 Holcombs, (Christy in place of Janice) along one side of the long table, and the 5 Beckers and Brent along the other side. Noah and Eleanor sat at the far end, and Joseph and Marge were at the end closest to the kitchen.

The meal was extra delicious and the conversation covered many topics, but the most interesting to all seemed to be the harrowing trip through the snowstorm. It did seem, however, that the afternoon was going by too quickly.

Liz and Josh finally slipped away to the library

for their rendezvous as everyone watched and smiled. David and Rachel knew the reason Liz wanted to talk to Josh so there was no concern on their faces. "Those two certainly know how to keep our telephone companies in business," David chuckled.

"I'll agree with that," Tom added, "my telephone bill is beginning to look like my feed bill." That, of course, caused the whole room to erupt in laughter.

"What would we do without young love?" Noah asked as his eyes sparkled and his gaze swept around the room. He was remembering how he had helped at least two of these couples make their decision to spend their life together as man and wife. He was still hoping that Brent would break down soon and make that decision with Susan. He'd left as soon as he'd finished eating to be with her and her parents for awhile. *Maybe he has a ring with him for a wonderful Thanksgiving present, Noah murmured to himself, or so* he'd thought.

"Did you say something, Noah?" Eleanor asked as she sat in a chair next to him. "I thought you mumbled something about a present. Would it be for me?" she giggled.

"No, Sweetheart, I was just thinking of a possible surprise happening today. Now don't ask me to tell you, because I can't divulge my secret thoughts," he chuckled.

"You and your secret thoughts are going to catch up with you one of these days, Mr. Hayes," she retorted while smiling at her beloved husband.

"I was only thinking how young love has, for such a long time, made the world a wonderful place to live and enjoy the finer things in life. Just look at the two of us. We started as young lovers and think of all the fun we've had for almost 52 years."

"You're right, of course, Noah, but we're two of the most exceptional people on earth," she laughed as she patted his cheek.

Jon and Christy, who'd recently celebrated their first month of married life, were sitting on the couch holding hands. They were grinning at the antics of Eleanor and Noah and then Jon gave her a quick kiss. "The world just wouldn't be the same without all the magic of young love" he whispered.

Chapter Five

When Josh and Liz reached the library, he opened his arms and she slipped into them as if she belonged. "I've missed this except in my dreams," he said as he lifted her chin and looked into those beautiful eyes. "Would you mind if I gave you a little kiss?"

"Well, you know, Josh, I'm not seventeen yet, and with my parents' restrictions I am really supposed to be untouched for another three months," she grinned. "That is really quite an outlandish rule, don't you think?"

"It might be a little over protective, but I respect their concern and I'll just give you a peck on the cheek. I don't want to get in trouble with your parents." he chuckled.

"Do you think I should let you steal another kiss like you did at the wedding?"

"I'm going to play it safe, Liz." He bent down to follow through with the kiss on her cheek, but her arms were suddenly around his neck. Her lips met his, gently but still rather passionately in a kiss which lingered long enough for Josh to put his arms around her and pull her into his embrace. He knew he shouldn't be doing this and finally held her at arm's length, shook his head in amazement, but also had to grin at her expression.

"That's more like it," she sighed as she dropped her hands to her sides and gave him a more than satisfied smile.

"Before you get any more ideas in that sneaky little head of yours, what is the favor you wanted to ask me, or has it already been completed?"

"No, it hasn't been completed. I thought we might talk a little bit before I have to humble myself and ask a ridiculous favor that you'll probably say no to anyway. But, if that's the way you want it, I'll get right to the point," she pouted.

"Hold it, Pipsqueak. I don't want to hurry anything. I'd be very happy to sit down on the couch over there and hold you, talk to you, and maybe even steal another kiss or two since you're being daring today." He raised his eyebrows in a teasing way, "but, I'd gotten the feeling that this was something you wanted to talk about right away."

Josh took her by the hand and headed for the couch. When they got seated, he put his arm around her shoulders and then turned to look into her eyes. "Well now, we're sort of aware of what we're both doing in school because of the e-mails and phone calls going back and forth. I guess I could tell you I've really missed holding you, dancing with you, and just looking at you for the six weeks since the wedding. I don't think you have the slightest idea what you do to me, Liz, whenever I hear the sound of your voice or see you in person anymore, and I don't know how I'm going to get through the rest of the school year without seeing you. Do you think that's enough of me baring my soul?" he chuckled.

"Josh, that was so sweet. I know you're just teasing me again and not the least bit serious, but it's still nice to hear. I'm sorry I have two years of school after this one. If I had my way, I would quit after this year, but Dad insists that I finish high school."

"How can you say that you'd quit school, Liz? You're smart, talented, so inquisitive about life, and enjoy different languages and cultures, I'd think you would really love going to school. What have you set as your goal in life, anyway?"

"I'm not going to embarrass myself by telling you that little piece of information, so I'd better just ask my favor. Please don't think you have to humor me, though, because I'll understand if you feel it's too far to drive or you have other plans while you're home."

"Liz, will you please just ask? What, exactly, would you like me to do while I'm at home? I may jump at the chance to do something a little different, if it's with you, because I'm afraid my home stay might get a little boring at times with no classes or school life to keep me occupied for almost six weeks."

"Oh, all right, Josh. My school is having a Christmas Formal on Friday, the 16th, and I wondered if you might agree to be my date, but I'm sure it's too much to ask."

"My sweet little Princess, you'd actually ask me to come to a Christmas Formal at your school when there are probably dozens of guys lining up to ask you?"

"Don't be funny, Josh. The guys in my school are such nerds, I'd rather stay home than go with one of them. I'm not even sure they know how to ask for a date."

"Is this a true formal, calling for me to get into a tux again?"

"You can wear a dress suit, if you'd rather. Mary says the guys come in either."

"Are you going to be wearing a formal or a street length dress?"

Grinning, but also blushing a little, she replied, "I'm actually planning to wear the same formal I wore at Christy's wedding."

"Oh, wow, I'll definitely need to be in a tux. You were beautiful in that gown."

"Thanks, Josh, but are you saying that you'll really consider it? I was all set to miss my first high school dance."

"Now, could I let that happen, Princess? Of course I'll consider being your date if you won't be embarrassed having an escort some will think is your uncle or older cousin."

"Is that the way you feel, Josh? Do you think of yourself more like my uncle or a cousin than a date or a friend? I definitely don't feel that way, since I've gotten to know you, but if you think you'd be self-conscience being there, then please don't agree to go."

"Elizabeth Becker," he laughed as he took her hand and kissed each finger. "I've adored you in so many ways, and right now I wish we were both through school. I'd love to tell the whole world that we're going to be together forever and ever. I can't believe my feelings sometimes because I didn't think I was ready for any serious relationship. That is, until I set eyes on you, and it didn't help any when I saw those looks Jon and Christy were exchanging at the wedding. I just couldn't shake the thought that I wanted the same thing with you some day. But, you are so young, Liz, and you still have so many teenage years ahead of you to enjoy. How about the trip to Spain that you might get to take with your Spanish class? Just think, you could meet a handsome Spaniard and promise to return to him after your graduation," he chuckled.

Liz turned to stare at him and to shake her head. "All right, Cupid, my handsome lover is waiting for me in Spain, but right now I need an escort to a formal dance in just three weeks. Are you going to save me from the tortures of asking one of those boring guys at school or maybe just staying at home? I'm sure I won't get asked by one I would actually accept a date with and then have to get a chaperone besides."

"Yes, Little Darlin', I'll be there in my tux, my shoes shined, and maybe even a few of my Christmas bells jingling all the way. Is Mary going to this dance, too?"

"She wouldn't miss her senior year Christmas formal. Of course, she'll also have her Senior Prom next Spring. She began dating Damon Roberts right after we started to school this Fall, and they seem to be getting pretty close. Luckily she was eighteen and could date without a chaperone all this year. His father's an Oncologist and Damon plans to go into the Medical field, also. He and Mary are in several classes together, and they do a lot of homework together, too. Dad knows his father so he approves." She smiled as she continued, "Dad feels he knows you, too, Josh, and he told me he would relax his rule of a chaperone if I was going to the dance with you. Even though he's still a little concerned about the age difference, he seems to trust you. I don't know for sure what he based that on--he apparently doesn't know you like I do," she giggled.

"Liz, I'm really flattered that your father trusts me to spend time with you, even if you don't, you little imp. However, even after bearing my soul a little bit ago, I can't see a future for us being in the cards. You know I'm planning to help Dad with the farm, and I won't even be in your league. This is what I've always wanted to do, work with the soil and raise animals. You know I love to ride, and I've taken classes to prepare myself for the task of handling all the situations on a farm. It isn't the best scenario for a city girl like you."

"I think I told you once, Josh Holcomb, but let me tell you again, that I would rather live at the ranch any day than in the city where I've had to grow up. I wish I could've gone to school here in Hayes and been a small town girl. My dream is to someday be a wife and a mother, and hopefully I'll be good at both. I'd love to live somewhere in the country, so don't ever say that a farm is not a good scenario for me." She then slapped her hands over her mouth and gasped, "I didn't mean to say that."

Chuckling, Josh replied, "Yes, Ma'am, I can see that those words just happened to slip out, but I'm so glad to know what you really want in life."

Just then they heard Tom calling Josh's name so they hurried back to the living room. "We'll have to be leaving pretty soon, Son, and I was wondering what your plans are. If you want to stay a few days here in Hayes, Jon says you're welcome to stay in the apartment he lived in before he and Christy were married. He'll be working days, but he's sure you can find things to keep yourself busy."

"I'd love to stay here for a few days, but would that be all right with you, Dad? If you need my help at the farm, I'll be glad to go back with you."

"I want your last year of college to be carefree and happy, Joshua. If you'd like to stay here and visit for two or three days, I'm sure Matthew and I can handle the farm duties. Janice has also been helping out just to be near Matthew. It's really fun to watch, but right now my biggest concern is about getting you home. I have several buyers coming this weekend and next week, as you're aware of, and I'm not sure when I can get away to come get you. I do have an idea, if Jon can help."

Jon, who was standing close by, approached the two of them. "Did I hear my name mentioned?"

"Yes, Jon. Joshua *would* like to stay here for a few days, but I was reminding him that I have buyers coming over the weekend and next week so I'm not sure when I could come get him. I think we could work something out, but I'd need you to take him to a car dealership so he can buy a used truck and drive it home. I've wanted to get one for a few weeks now so Matthew can do some of the errands. I hate to have my truck gone from the farm, and I don't want him using his car for my errands."

"Sure, we can do that. In fact, I've passed a dealership right close to where you get on the highway north of here. I can check with Joseph or Brent about its reputation. What type did you have in mind?"

"I'd like just a small pickup, something like the Chevy S-10 or a small Dodge. I'd prefer it to be no more than five years old, not an enormous amount of miles, and hopefully just a one owner. I'll give you a check to take care of it, and I presume the dealer will know how to ensure it has a temporary license and some insurance until Josh gets it back home. In fact, I'll give you the farm insurance card and it can be added to that with the same coverage as the others."

"I'll check Colorado laws, but I think a person has so many hours or days to apply for license and insurance, as long as you have proof of purchase, but is there a little more information on your card than we have on ours? And that reminds me, I need to transfer my coverage to the Law Firm policy--possibly at the next renewal. Noah talked to me about that recently."

"O.K., I'll let you know when the renewal comes up. Yours or Joshua's card will have all the information you'll need now. I'd forgotten about that and also that I now have a son to handle the legal matters," he chuckled. "Well, if that's settled, I think I'll get your mother and Jacob and head home. I'm relying on you to keep an eye on your brother, Jon. I think he is really trying hard to change his attitude about a few things, since he witnessed an accident that I'll let him tell you about, but it will most likely take some time. Can you take us to the plane in a few minutes?"

"I sure can. Just let me tell Christy where I'm going."

Tom turned to Josh who had just returned from talking to Liz again. "I'll just be my repetitious self now and remind you to behave yourself, Joshua. This is a great family, and Jon doesn't need any one of us causing problems in his job or his marriage."

"I'm learning real fast about this family, Dad, and you don't need to worry. My life was definitely changed after experiencing that accident the other day and finding the baby unharmed, not to mention this chance to see Liz again," he chuckled. "I do want to thank you and Mom for letting me find God in my own way, or maybe His way, and I'll be extra careful driving the truck home, too." He then gave his dad a big hug.

Chapter Six

The snow had quit falling completely around 1 o'clock and the sun had come out in all its glory. The hired hands had cleared most of the snow off the runway and the sun had done a good job of melting the rest. Tom would have no problem taking off. Josh decided to ride with Jon to the plane, say goodbye to his mom and to Jacob, and also grab his bag with the few clothes he had stuffed into it just in case he was lucky enough to get to stay a few days with his big brother. He hadn't really been sure if Jon would want him around after just one month of marriage, but he'll try not to interfere, especially if Liz is still here.

It had seemed strange not to see Janice with the family, but he guessed she was also growing up. *This infatuation with Matthew is something new, but I wonder if she is as taken with Matthew as I am with Liz. Maybe Jon started a snowball rolling down a steep hill when he saw Christy on that plane and felt he heard God telling him that she was the one He had picked for him. I've certainly discovered that God has miracles in store for each of us if we'll just listen, and I'm determined to do that from now on.*

There were plenty of leftovers to enjoy when the sun started going down. Jon, with Christy, Josh and Liz decided to pack some food and ride out toward the mountains. It had been timed just right for them to see the most beautiful red sky at sunset. Christy led them to a huge boulder that made a perfect table for their basket of food and enough space so the four of them could sit around the edge. It was a perfect evening although they were glad they had all worn warm jackets and caps, and were also wearing their riding gloves.

The turkey sandwiches, chips and relishes were delicious, but, to their surprise, Christy had brought a whole cherry pie. She laughingly said, "Mom is going to wonder what happened to this pie, but there's still two or three left for the rest of them." She had cut it, before she packed it in the carrier, and brought a spatula to lift the pieces out onto the paper plates she had also tucked in.

"Are we going to eat this with our fingers, or has my wonderful efficient wife also thought to put some forks in her magic basket?" Jon had tried to whisper, but Josh and Liz had heard him and started giggling.

"I am here to fulfill your every wish, my dear," Christy smirked as she pulled four forks out of the basket. "It is magic, you see, that this basket can almost always produce the things you want, even things to keep you warm." She'd started laughing and Jon had to join in since he could never forget their trip to the State Park on his birthday back in June. Christy had one of his birthday presents tucked in the bottom of the basket. It had been a heating pad to keep him warm in bed. She had given him the little kitten that day, too, that was supposed to keep him warm, but that little ball of fur has never come close to the bed.

He had really wanted the 'heat transfer' which she'd given him the day Noah had thought he might be coming down with the flu. Noah had sent her up to his apartment to make sure he was warm, had enough aspirins, and to fix him some soup. She'd found him in bed but shivering, and the only way she knew to get him warm was to get in bed with him and transfer her heat to him like she'd read in a book. That had been so nice to wake up to and had actually started their closer relationship.

"Well, there must be a private joke there," Josh said, "but I think Liz and I will just enjoy this pie. Thanks, Christy, for all the trouble you went to."

"When we finish eating, I'd like to show Josh the lake and cabin where the men stay when they come out to hunt deer or pheasants," Liz remarked. "Would that be OK?"

"I think we should be heading back. Liz. It's starting to get a little dark. Since I'm going to stay for a few days, maybe you could show me that tomorrow or Saturday," Josh replied.

"Oh, I guess it would be better to see it in the daytime. It was so much fun when we girls used to sneak out there and play. I think it was the first time we came, we hadn't told our parents where we were going. We stayed until almost dark, and by the time we got back, they were frantic and furious," Liz laughed.

"We paid for that little episode, if I remember correctly. At least I did," Christy chimed in. "I had to help clean the stalls for a week."

"That was a very good lesson," Jon chuckled. "Josh and I did our recompense the time we were caught by the sheriff speeding on the highway between our home and that little town of Lamar. We were teenagers just trying to see how fast we could get Dad's car to go. Do you remember that, Josh?"

"How could I forget? Dad made us work like

slaves, and every time we needed to go somewhere, we'd had to ask Mom to take us because we couldn't touch the car for a whole month. I remember doing quite a bit of walking, too. Yeah, we learned a real good lesson, all right, and our friends had a good laugh on us. The only downer was that you were driving because you were 17 and I was only 12, but I worked as hard as you did."

"Knowing you, Josh, you probably talked your way out of a lot of the work. If I remember correctly, your chores were in the horse barn, but I had to work out in the hog confinement. You were probably talking to Moonlight most of the time."

"Not so. Moonlight wasn't even born then, but Dad was standing right beside me most of the time. He'd said, 'I want you to learn how to do everything correctly so I don't have to teach you again.' Day after day, I had to do the same thing whether it was a daily job or a weekly one, or even a monthly one."

"It must not have discouraged you very much since that's the job you're studying to take over some day."

They'd all gotten a big bang out of the tales, but then they realized just how dark it had gotten. "We'd better get back to the house pronto before we're all doing chores again! Dad is going to be upset, I'm sure," Christy exclaimed a little frightened.

Christy led the way as she was more familiar with the trails, but she soon realized that she hadn't been out when it was this dark, at least that she could remember. She then decided to let Rainbow have the rein, and he expertly led them home.

Their parents had definitely been concerned, and Brent and Brad were getting ready to start out to look for them. Christy received a rather stern look from her dad as he said, "I thought you knew better than to stay out there so late, Christy. Did you let Rainbow or one of the other horses bring you home?"

Christy felt ashamed and knew that her face was turning red. "To be honest, I did let Rainbow have the rein, but the time just got away from us, Dad. We were telling tales of our childhoods, and we got so engrossed that we didn't realize it was getting so dark."

"I just ask that each of you take a little more responsibility for the safety of all the others with you when you're out like that. All four of you know the hazards of a farm or ranch, and I expect you to heed them. Is that understood?"

Nodding, they all felt that they had deserved the very short lecture from Joseph so promised to be much more conscience of where they were and what they were doing.

Chapter Seven

Josh was so happy to be in Hayes again. He had, he was afraid, fallen in love with the town and wished there were some way he could actually live here. He was dreaming big, of course, because he knew his future was at the family farm, and it was what he had studied for the last four years. It's just that Jon and Christy seem to make everything so exciting, and it is such a great little town with so many more things to do than down on the farm, so to speak.

He remembers, when Jon and Christy returned from their honeymoon, they hadn't forgotten their vow to help the Gulf Coast hurricane victims in some way. They'd appealed to the residents of Hayes for money donations for the Red Cross, and it had been a very generous outpouring. Jon and Christy had then loaded the back of their Tahoe with all kinds of things, from health bars, crackers with cheese, boxed crackers to hold peanut butter, Gatorade and bottled water, dried and canned fruit with pull tabs lids, to the plastic spoons and knives, Handy Wipes, suntan lotion, Chap Stick, as well as deodorants, shampoo, soap, toothbrushes, toothpaste and combs for personal hygiene. They'd made the trip down to New Orleans, and they had come back with the Lambre family of five, including the parents, Erick and Carole, and the three kids, Jaclyn, Grant, and Phillip.

Through the handling of an estate, Jon knew of a house and its contents that were to be auctioned in the near future. The heirs had taken the things they'd wanted and the rest was now ready to be resolved. Jon had talked to Noah by phone from New Orleans and a deal was made with the executor to let them buy it lock, stock, and barrel. It was a three bedroom ranch style home with a full basement and a nice large back yard. There was an extra large master bedroom with a queen-size bed and sitting area. One of the other bedrooms had twin beds so the two boys, Grant, twelve, and Phillip, ten, could share until some rooms could be partitioned off in the basement. The third room was a little smaller and had been a home office. All of those items had been taken by the family, so the almost sixteen-year-old daughter, Jaclyn, got to pick out her own furniture and she was so thrilled. A few pieces had been taken from the living room, but there was enough left for them to comfortably get by until they could buy what they wanted. All the appliances were left in the kitchen, along with quite a few dishes and pans, which really delighted Carole.

Noah and Jon also helped them find jobs. Erick had been an electrician in the New Orleans area, so Hayes Electrical Shop, the Appliance Store, and Custom Lighting could all use his services. Since they were in close proximity, it was decided that the owner of the Electrical Shop would actually hire him and the other two would pay for his services when they needed him. Erick was elated.

His wife, Carole, although she had not worked previously, wanted to help at least for a little while until they got back on their feet. She was asked if she would like to work in the lunch room at the school that the two boys would be attending. It pleased her that she could be there to help the children adjust to their new home, the town and the school. This had all been done before Thanksgiving, and they are all doing really great according to Jon and Christy.

❧

Friday morning Josh caught Jon before he went down to the office. "Hey, Jon, do you think I could borrow the Tahoe to go to the ranch? I was hoping

Liz would go riding with me, show me that cabin, and then, maybe, we could all go to a movie tonight. What do ya think?"

"I think, maybe, you should avoid any scandal or speculations about your intentions toward Liz by staying away from that cabin until Christy and I can go with you. She and I were discussing that last night and we thought, perhaps, about riding out there tomorrow. We'll fix a picnic lunch that we'll eat at the cabin, and we can have the fireplace going to make it nice and cozy. We could possibly come back and play some doubles in tennis, if the weather gets warm like it's forecast, but it may be a little chilly for that. A movie sounds good."

Chuckling, he continued, "You'd better call and see what kind of reception you get from whomever answers, then talk to Liz. Maybe you could pick her up and we'll all have lunch together here in town, and I have a couple of errands you could do for me before you go to the ranch. Do you know what's playing at the movie?"

"No, I don't, and you're right, as usual, about the cabin. Liz seems to be so trusting, and I certainly wouldn't take advantage of her, but it might not look so good to the rest of the family, especially since she told me she couldn't date until she's eighteen. Oh, now I get it. Her parents did whisper in your ear, didn't they?"

he chuckled. "O.K., what do you need me to do, and should they be done before or after I talk to Liz?"

"Go ahead and call Liz about 9 o'clock and then come on down to the office. I need you to go to the Farm Supply Store for some Kitty Litter and also to the Jewelry Store. My wedding ring was tight when Christy put it on my finger, and I need to have it stretched just a bit. I'm lucky my waistbands were a little loose because they're getting a little snug now, too. I'm trying not to let Christy know because she may quit feeding me."

"I thought you looked a little heavier than you used to. I didn't know six weeks of marriage could make that much difference. You'd better come over and use your own nice and handy treadmill." He had a big grin on his face as he said, "I remember Christy saying something about you becoming like Santa Claus or Wilt Chamberlain, and it sure looks like it's leaning toward Santa. Ho, Ho, Ho." Chuckling, he started toward the door to the deck where he would jump over the railings to the other apartment. He'd just decided to use the treadmill himself for a little bit before calling Liz. *If guys gain weight that quickly after they get married, I'd better be plenty thin and muscular before it happens. I wonder how Dad has stayed so thin. I suppose the kind of work you do makes a difference. I'm glad I'll be on the farm like Dad.*

Jon, however, gave one last order before Josh reached the door. "Josh, keep all this just between us two or you may not be invited to stay here anymore. Understand?"

"I got ya. I'll see you later."

Josh got Liz on the phone without a problem, and she was excited about coming to town for lunch. "I'll be ready at 11 o'clock sharp so don't be late," she giggled. She'd then hesitantly asked, "Josh, ah--would you consider going shopping with me after we've eaten?" His hesitation got her to laughing, but she'd continued in a whisper, "I'll wait and tell you about it when I see you. Too many ears around here and I want it to be a surprise." Back in her regular voice, she said, "By the way, Dad and Mary went home this morning. Dad has a patient he's quite concerned about, and Mary has a date with Damon tonight. Mom isn't sure when she'll go, but she thinks she'll stay until Sunday."

"I sure hope so, since I'm going to be here with nothing to do while Jon and Christy work today and Monday. I did mention to Jon that maybe we could go to a movie tonight, so if you want to bring a change of clothes, we'll probably eat out again before we do that. Well, I guess that's it. I'll see you at 11 o'clock. Bye for now."

"I didn't hear being personally invited to go to

the movie, but I'll assume that I am as long as I'm supposed to bring other clothes." Giggling, she broke the connection.

Josh stared at the phone and shook his head. *That saying is definitely true about women. We can't live with them and we certainly can't survive without them. What are we poor men to do? She was right about the invitation, though. I'd better watch my manners around that little gal. She doesn't miss a chance to remind me of my shortcomings.*

He went to the office and found Jon, luckily, without a client. Jon tugged at his ring until he finally got it off. Just as he was handing it to Josh, who should appear at the door but Christy. "Hey, Josh, what's on your schedule today?"

Quickly putting his hand in his pocket, he said, "Jon has asked me to go to the Farm Supply for him. I guess Sub needs a clean litter box. Then I'm going to the ranch to pick up Liz and bring her to town. Jon and I thought we'd take you lovely ladies to lunch, if that fits your day's schedule. Liz mentioned some shopping she wanted to do after lunch, and she coerced me into going with her. I have no idea what that's about."

"I think I do," she grinned. "Her dad's birthday is coming up and she did mention to me that she'd like to get something different for him this year and make it her own surprise. She usually has to go with her mom and Mary to pick something out from all of them. Your plan sounds cool for lunch so I'll see you both later. Jon, Sweetie, I have to go now to the library for a few minutes. I love you."

"Love you, too, Christy." He waited until he'd heard the door open and shut.

"Whew, that was close. Here's some money to pay for the Kitty Litter, but you'll have to take my credit card for the ring. Do you think they could have it ready before we go to lunch?"

"I doubt it, Jon. Why don't you just tell Christy you have to get it made larger? She'd understand. I don't think married folk should have secrets from each other."

"You wouldn't understand, but it's just too soon. Maybe I can run up and get my class ring and turn it around so I can get through lunch."

"And how, may I ask, do you expect me to pick up your ring this afternoon with Liz right there beside me? Do you have an answer for that, Big Brother?"

"Problems, problems. Just give me my credit card back. I'll get away some way this afternoon and pick it up myself."

"What needs to be picked up? Maybe I can help." Jon and Josh both turned to see Noah standing there smiling and waiting for a reply.

"Oh. .ah. .Noah. No, that's all right. Josh is

dropping something off for me but I'll pick it up this afternoon because Liz has asked him to do some shopping with her."

"Oh, tell her I need a new pen for my desk or a new tie. That's what I get every year for Christmas so I might as well want it, right?" He chuckled as he glanced at Jon.

Jon, of course, had forgotten to hide his ring hand and Noah's eyes are a little too sharp. "Is Christy around?" He came into the office and closed the door. "I see your ring is missing, Jon. It's gotten too small already, huh? I wondered how long yours would last when I saw Christy struggling to get it on your finger at the wedding. Well, you beat me by about 2 months, but mine was too large when Eleanor put it on *my* finger.

It must come with the territory, Son, now that you're sitting most of the day with a pen in that hand since you're left handed. Your wife is over-feeding you because she wants to impress you with her great cooking skills, but I think I may have a solution. I happen to have my first ring in my desk because I had to buy a new one. They couldn't even stretch that one enough to fit, and to find a new one to match was impossible because Eleanor had bought it up in Estes Park at some specialty shop. She'd loved the ring, but had known it was too small, so she'd had them stretch it before the wedding.

76

How do I know that, you ask? Eleanor knew immediately that I had a new ring on and figured out what had happened, so we talked about it. You can't fool your wife about very much, Jon, but this may be worth a try. Anyway, you can probably wear mine and get by until you pick yours up this afternoon. Of course, that is only if you can keep your hand out of Christy's sight," he chuckled.

"Now, we'd better let Josh get on his way because I need to talk to you before our next client comes in."

"I'm out of here. Have a nice day, Mr. Hayes, and I'll see you at noon, Jon." As Josh left the offices, he thought to himself, "That is one cool guy." Then he remembered that Liz had told him that he and Noah had the same birthday, and he couldn't keep a smile off his face or wondering if he could ever be that clever.

Chapter Eight

By the time Josh had finished the errands and then stopped to buy a soft drink, it was about 11:05 when he got to the ranch. Liz was waiting and, of course, decided to tease him on being late. "Did you go back to sleep after you called me?" she giggled.

"You're so funny, Pretty Lady. My big brother had a few errands for me to do this morning that took longer than I had expected. I'm terribly sorry I'm a whole five minutes late, but just remember I'll be checking my watch very closely when I come to pick you up for this Christmas formal," he replied in friendly sarcasm.

She laughed, "We'll see who's late for the dance. You'll have that long drive and I'll have all afternoon to primp and get dressed. Now that you've challenged me, I'll definitely see that I'm ready early. I just realized, though, that you're probably planning to stay with Christy and Jon the night before so you won't have so far to drive. Am I right?"

"I'm not telling."

With the friendly bickering, they were back in town before they realized it. They'd enjoyed watching the last of the leaves floating down from the trees, covering the sides of the road and beginning to fill the ditches. It looked like a multi-colored quilt inviting you to lie down and rest.

"We have a few minutes before Jon and Christy will join us," Josh said as he pulled the Tahoe back into Jon's parking space at the Law Firm. "We could walk over and sit in Jeremiah Park, if you'd like, and you could tell me what we're going to be shopping for this afternoon."

"Oh, yes, let's go to the park. It's such a pretty day, and with the bright sunshine to warm things up, I don't think we'll get too cold. I'd almost forgotten that you'd agreed to go with me to do some shopping. It's awfully nice of you, Josh, to be my shopping companion and consultant. My problem is getting something for my dad. His birthday is December 4, and every year Mom, Mary and I go traipsing around downtown Colorado Springs to buy a gift from all of us. I'd like to give him a small gift from just me this year, but I'm not sure what to get. I thought you might have some suggestions."

"Well, before I forget a message I'm supposed to pass on to you, Noah said to tell you he needs a new pen for his desk or a new tie. So, that takes care of Christmas for him. Now, let's see, what does your dad like to do away from the office? Does he golf? Does he fish? I know he plays tennis, swims, and rides horses. Is there anything else?"

"Did Grandpa Noah really say that, Josh? I'll have to make sure he doesn't get one of those gifts this Christmas. We probably have stocked him up on those two items," she let out a giggle. "As for Dad, I would never have thought of sports items. Mom always goes to the Men's Clothing Department and we settle for a nice shirt and tie. Sometimes we'll splurge and get him a new sports jacket. I love your suggestions, Josh, so we'll start by looking in the sports section at the Mercantile." She then glanced toward the office door and jumped up as she exclaimed, "Oh, here come Christy and Jon. Let's go, I'm really starved."

As Jon and Christy approached, Josh asked, "Hey, you guys, Liz says she's starved, so do you think we can afford to take her with us to lunch?"

"Maybe this once, but we'll have to make sure she eats a good breakfast next time so we won't go broke." Jon had cleverly gone along with the tease.

"You're as big a tease as your brother, Jon, and here I thought you were a nice guy," Liz retorted. "I'll just pay for my own lunch if you two are going to be stingy today."

"Will you pay for mine, too?" Josh laughed as he took her hand and pulled her along.

They walked to the Cafe on the southeast corner of Main Street and South Broad, and were seated in the corner windows. It gave a perfect view of the old historic Broad Street Hotel on the northwest corner and its outstanding landscaping for almost a block to the north. In the mostly shaded parking lot, across Broad Street to the west, they could see the sunshine filtering through a few rather large evergreen trees and the now bare limbs of the deciduous trees. It gives a nice ethereal setting to the area as it extends over to Jefferson Street, and also provides much needed parking for sports events, movies, and shopping.

Jon started the conversation by asking, "Josh, have you given any more thought to when we should go look for that truck for Dad?"

"Oh, Dear Lord, I had completely forgotten we had to get transportation for me to get home. Do you have any idea when you can go?"

"Well, I was thinking that if we got up and went to the dealership fairly early in the morning, we could get that done before noon and it most likely will have warmed up a little, too. Then, we could go riding in the afternoon, take a look at that cabin, and possibly have a little snack there before riding back. Dinner and the evening are up for grabs."

"I might have known there'd have to be eating there someplace," Christy laughed. "I am definitely going to put you on a diet, Mr. Holcomb, because you're putting on too much weight. I've noticed your pants are getting a little tighter around the waist, and if you're not careful, you'll be having those love handles. I think your ring is getting too tight for your finger already, too. I remember my struggle getting it on your finger at the wedding."

"You don't need to rub it in, Christy." He tucked his left hand in his lap hoping she wouldn't notice his missing ring. "I'll promise to start using the treadmill again, and you can challenge me to jog more on our walks."

"Aren't you wearing your ring, Jon? Just what were you handing Josh this morning when I stopped at your office door?" Looking over at Josh with an inquisitive smile, she asked, "Do you have anything to say, Josh?"

"Not a word. As I said then, Jon asked me to do an errand for him, and he was just giving me some money to pay for that. He also gave me the keys to the Tahoe, but I think that was after you'd left."

"You brothers stick together like that Crazy Glue, but Liz and I will find out the truth, won't we, Liz?"

"I don't know anything about the ring situation, but I *am* interested in going to buy a truck tomorrow morning for Josh to drive home. What's the story behind this, and do I get to go help pick something out? It sounds like so much fun, and I've never ever been to a car dealership before."

"Well, Christy usually wants to clean the apartment on Saturday mornings, so it was going to be just Josh and me, but it's fine if you, or both of you, want to go."

"Would you want to go, Christy? I love doing different things, and it always seems to be here in Hayes that I get the chance." She hesitated a second because of the puzzled look on Christy's face. "Christy, is something wrong?"

"Well, I'm not sure. This is the first I'd heard of buying a truck for their dad. When did this plan originate and why haven't you said anything about it before now, Jon?" She gave a rather cool stare at her husband.

"I'm sorry, Sweetheart. Before the folks left yesterday, when Josh decided he'd like to stay for a few days, Dad said that was fine, but he wasn't sure when he could come and get him. He has buyers coming in tomorrow and next week, and he has to be prepared for them. He said he'd been wanting to get a small pickup truck so Matthew could do some of the daily errands without using Dad's truck and leaving him without transportation. He'd then had this suggestion that maybe I could take Josh to a dealership to buy a truck and Josh could drive it on home. I guess it just slipped my mind until this morning when Josh asked about going to the ranch and bringing Liz in for lunch. I'm really sorry, Sweetie." He reached over and ran his fingers down her cheek as he wiggled his eyebrows at her.

"Oh, forget it, You Charmer. I can understand how, with all the confusion around there yesterday and getting your folks to the airstrip, it could've slipped your mind. I just don't want things to be kept from me, unless of course, it's going to be a nice surprise for me personally," she giggled. She leaned over and gave him a little kiss on the cheek. "Now, to answer your question, Liz, I'll be up and ready to go. It does sound like a fun adventure, but what time does 'early' mean, Jon? Do you have any idea when this place opens?"

"I called Brent this morning after Noah and I had finished with our client. He said that Fred Moore lives here in Hayes but decided to open the dealership up on the highway because he felt he would draw more customers up there. He is very reliable and carries several makes of cars and trucks, new and used. He opens at 6:00 a.m. every day except on Sunday when he's closed until 2:00 p.m."

"I know Fred and he's a great guy," Christy remarked. "I haven't seen him for awhile because he's most likely at the dealership every day. He has two boys, if I recall, who would be old enough now to be working with him."

Josh spoke up. "Well, I guess we have all the information we need, so what time do you think we should plan to take off? I really wouldn't think we'd have to be there when he opens, would we? I don't particularly like the idea of getting up that early." he chuckled.

"If we want to go riding in the afternoon, we'll probably want to get away by 8:30. You can never tell how long those papers will take to fill out, and we certainly don't want to buy the first truck we look at. We'll want to drive at least one, check under the hood, and all that stuff you're supposed to do when you're negotiating a deal for a used car or truck. If we can get up there by 9:00, we should have plenty of time to get that done by noon."

"Believe it or not, I didn't hear a word about getting something to eat before, during or after we close the deal. How about that, guys?" Christy got to laughing so hard she had tears running down her cheeks.

"It's not really that funny, Christy. So I like to eat all that wonderful food you've been fixing for me, and, in fact, I had mentioned having a snack at the cabin. Maybe you'll just have to start serving smaller portions. If you go and put me on a diet, though, I'll probably become a crab, you won't love me anymore, and I'll just end up crawling down to the lake to pine away." He gave her that grin that just melts her heart, and she had to have a kiss.

"That's enough already, you two. Let's stick to business for a few minutes and try to figure out how and when we'll pick up Liz."

"One of the roads that can take us to the highway goes right by the ranch, so Liz can jump in as we're driving by. You can do that, can't you, Liz?" Jon chuckled.

"Certainly, I'll put a trampoline by the side of the road and just bounce myself right into the car," she laughingly retorted.

"I was always told that I was the clown in the family, but I think I'm the only sober one in this group today," Josh smirked. "What did you guys slip into your drinks anyway?"

"You just need a little time, Josh. You're sure to catch up, but maybe your thoughts are dwelling on the big shopping spree you're going on this afternoon with Liz. Your funny bone hasn't kicked in yet today." Jon was still chuckling as they left the cafe and started to walk down Main Street, which, of course, took them right past the Jewelry Store.

"What time is your ring supposed to be ready, Sweetheart?" Christy whispered as she was smiling mischievously. She'd cleverly managed to walk on Jon's left side, and without a conscience thought, Jon had taken her hand in his. She'd quickly pulled it toward her face to take a look at the ring he was wearing before he'd realized what he'd done.

"Oh, Christy, how do you always know how to find out all my secrets?"

"It's just one of the many tricks of being a wife who loves her very handsome friend and husband, Sweetheart." She tenderly reached up and gave him a pat on his cheek.

"Noah warned me about wives this morning, but as long as you know, let's stop at the Jewelry Store now and see if they have it finished. Do you two want to stop with us, or are you anxious to get your shopping started? A piece of jewelry might be a nice present for your dad, Liz."

"I don't think so this year. Josh has already suggested a couple of things that I'm really excited about. We'll see you guys later." She took Josh's hand, while looking at him with the cutest smile, and started to pull him down the street.

"Hey, Cutie Pie, we've got all afternoon so we don't need to run and knock people down in our haste." He pulled her back beside him, put his arm across her shoulders, and even gave her a little kiss on the forehead.

"Josh, we're on Main Street," she scolded. They'd just reached the corner of York Street where they would cross Main Street to go to the Mercantile. Josh had instead turned south on York Street, walked a little ways along the side of the Jewelry Store, and then just stopped and turned to face her.

"Now we're not on Main Street," he grinned as his fingers gently tilted her chin so he could put a real kiss on her lips. He was surprised when she'd willingly responded, and so he'd stood back to watch as her face turned a scarlet red. He had to chuckle, though, when she was glaring at him.

"I hate you, Josh Holcomb."

"No, you don't, Liz. That cute little smile you gave me when we left Jon and Christy back there, and the response I got just now from that kiss tells me something very different. Come on now, and let's go shopping."

Chapter Nine

Liz soon forgot her embarrassment about the kiss because she was so thrilled with the shopping, and Josh was being such a superb help. She'd stopped at several counters to look at different items. She'd checked out the men's cologne, a sterling money clip, and even a nice scarf, but Josh finally guided her to the sports section of the Mercantile. She'd spent quite a while at the sports attire, but when Josh got her to look at the unusual items for the golfer, she found an insulated bottle holder that would fasten to a golf bag, on a golf cart, or even on a saddle that made her eyes sparkle. When the clerk mentioned that it could even be taken to the tennis court, on a boat, or to a favorite fishing spot, she was sold. She also added a package of three golf balls, a tube of tennis balls, and a fishing lure.

"I know it's December, but Dad is always complaining about being thirsty on the golf course and also the tennis court, so this will be great. He can put it away until Spring if he wants, but there could be a nice warm day when he can use it sooner than that. Thank you so very much, Josh, for your help."

"No problem, Princess. I am always ready to help a lady in distress." When they'd gotten outside on the sidewalk again, Josh asked, "Would you like to look for anything else, or should we mosey over to the cafe and get something to quench our dry mouths?"

"There *is* one other thing I would like to look for and maybe you can help me with that, too. You mentioned Grandpa jokingly listing his wants for Christmas, but would you have any ideas for what I could get him?"

"I was afraid I'd stuck my foot in my mouth when I conveyed his message to you, but I do have an idea I think he might really appreciate. I noticed yesterday that he kept pulling his coat collar up around his ears in that wind. I just happened to be looking out the window when he and Eleanor were coming over for Thanksgiving dinner, and he didn't have anything on his head, so I was wondering if he'd wear a cap with ear flaps that could be pulled down when it's cold out. He could definitely use it at the ranch if he wants to take a ride on Thunder and it's a chilly day."

"Oh, Josh, I love you!" She stood on tiptoe and kissed him on the cheek right there on the Main Street sidewalk.

"You told me earlier that you hated me, Liz, for kissing you *off* Main Street, so who's being a little too spontaneous now?" Josh chuckled as he put his hands on her shoulders and held her away from him.

"Oh, that was just an appreciation kiss," she laughed although her face was again a little too red. "Grandpa used to wear caps at the ranch a lot, so let's go to the Men's Store and see if we can find one. But what if they come in different sizes?"

"His head looks pretty average to me for his height and weight. I'll try them on and if they fit me, I'm sure they'll fit him. He can always exchange the one you buy, if it doesn't fit, after Christmas."

So off they went on another search, and they were lucky to find a nice selection of hats and caps at the Men's Store. They had to sort through several stacks of different styles, but they finally found just what they wanted. In fact, they found a sports cap for at the ranch and a dress cap for the office, church, etc. Liz was so excited she started to kiss him again at the check-out counter, but Josh stopped her this time. "Whoa, Little Lady, it's not the time or place," he whispered. "We can get to that later." Chuckling, he put his hand at the small of her back and guided her forward to the waiting clerk, who had a big smile on her face.

"It appears you had good luck in finding a Christmas present today. I imagine they must be for someone very special. I've heard that we're supposed to be getting more snow this year than we have for quite a while, so those caps could really come in handy. Would you like them to be wrapped for you or is that something you like to do yourself? Everyone is different in that area, it seems."

Liz was rather shy, all of a sudden, but as she handed the clerk her credit card, she explained that Josh had been a wonderful help to her in finding gifts for her dad and also her grandfather, and she'd love wrapping the gifts herself.

With their shopping completed, they headed toward the cafe for something to drink. "I'm sorry if I embarrassed you, Josh. I was so excited about the presents you helped me find that I just wanted to hug you."

"A hug may have been permissible, but I think you were heading for a little more than a hug at the Men's Store. I'm looking forward to claiming that kiss, however, during the dark cool movie tonight. How does that sound?"

"We'll see," she replied rather defiantly. "I may remember that I'm still just sixteen and you can't kiss me again until I'm seventeen."

"Your rules seem to change at will, Princess, and waiting until you're seventeen for another kiss just isn't going to happen. There's at least one occasion between now and then that requires you to be kissed, and that's your Christmas formal. You aren't going to deny me that pleasure, I can assure you."

"Have you looked at your watch? It's almost 4 o'clock and about time for Jon and Christy to be through for the day. Shall we head back to the office?"

With a big hearty laugh, Josh reached for her hand and headed for the door of the cafe. "Don't be thinking that changing the subject is going to help you, Princess, because I'm going to have a kiss that night for sure. There's still tonight and tomorrow, too, and who can tell---I may do something that will cause you to kiss me like you did this afternoon."

"You started the whole thing with that crazy trick down there by the Jewelry Store. It's a good thing Christy didn't see that or you would've been in big trouble."

"You really think so?" he chuckled, and he was still chuckling when they reached the office. Christy and Jon were just clearing their desks for the day, and they soon headed up to the apartment. Jon and Josh jumped over the railings to the other apartment to work out on the treadmill while Christy and Liz showered and changed clothes. Jon came back to shower and told them that Josh was cleaning up in the other apartment.

Liz played with Sub while Christy relaxed with a soda, and Jon and Josh joined them shortly. They enjoyed a few snacks and made their plans for the evening. They would eat at the Pub & Grub restaurant before the movie. It is such a fun place to go for an evening out, and neither Josh nor Liz had been there. With its good food, live music on Friday and Saturday nights, a nice dance floor, a few pinball machines, and even a dart board for testing your skills, people come and spend hours there. It had been a great addition to Hayes.

After eating, they were enjoying the band music, dancing, and sipping another soda so much that they forgot to watch the time. When Josh finally checked his watch, he looked at Liz and asked, "Did you do this on purpose, Miss Becker, so I couldn't get my kiss during the movie?"

"Oh, is it too late to go? I was having such a great time I didn't pay any attention to my watch. Aren't you having a good time, Josh? I think this is much more fun than a movie would've been. Just sitting and listening to the music, watching the people dance, and enjoying my drink like on a date, is something I've never done before."

"I can just imagine," he grinned at her. "Well, to me it doesn't make any difference whether it's in the movie or on the dance floor, because I'm going to get my kiss. Let's dance, Little Mysterious Princess."

"Josh, you can't kiss me on the dance floor. What will people think?"

"You didn't seem to worry about that this afternoon right on Main Street, My Little Darlin', so let's go," he chuckled. "I can pick you up and carry you out there if I have to."

"But- -ah- -there weren't all these people around then, Josh." Her face was turning a little red once again.

"What's the problem and what about all these people being around?" Jon asked as he and Christy came back to the table.

"Oh, Liz is trying to give me a hard time about dancing again since we realized we'd missed the movie. I was just telling her that I could carry her to the dance floor if I had to."

"He would just love to do that, too, Liz. I remember when he was in high school and he wanted to dance with a cute little classmate. She didn't think she wanted to leave her select group of friends, so Josh just picked her up, threw her over his shoulder and took her to the dance floor. You have to watch this guy because he can be very impulsive." Jon was trying to check his laughing at the memory when Josh lifted Liz into his arms and headed toward the dance floor to collect his kiss.

"But, wa-wanting to dan-dance isn't. . . . . . She didn't get to finish as Josh had put her down on the dance floor, quickly took her in his arms, and was holding her too, too close as he moved to the slow music. "Please, Josh, you're squeezing me way too tight." With no success whatsoever, she still kept protesting as she tried to wiggle free. Josh, however, had her secure in his arms and was enjoying her struggle as he prepared for his kiss.

He finally loosened his hold just a little as he whispered, "I can't let you get away, Liz, because I have at least a quick little kiss coming. Why don't you calm down and enjoy it like you did this afternoon beside the Jewelry Store?"

"There weren't all these people around then, and how do you know I enjoyed it?"

"Oh, Liz, you may only be sixteen, but you returned my kiss this afternoon and it was definitely one that was being enjoyed," he chuckled.

∽

"I never would've thought those two would still be friends after the way he kept up the teasing on the first day they met," Christy commented as they stood watching. "Liz was usually so reserved, but he's brought out a side of her that I had never seen. It's really fun to watch, but I still wonder if anything serious can come of it with the difference in their ages."

"We'll just have to trust God again, Christy."

Jon and Christy continued to watch the two as they danced so perfectly together--almost as if they were professionals. "How do you suppose they do that when they haven't danced together, that I know of, except at our wedding?" Christy asked.

"One explanation," Jon chuckled, "might be how tightly Josh is holding her. Maybe she can't do anything but follow his every step."

"Maybe you should try that, Dear. I might be less apt to step on your toes."

"I'd love to hold you that tight, Sweetie, but not necessarily out on the dance floor."

"Why, Jon Holcomb, I'm surprised at you," she exclaimed with a grin on her face.'

"Just wait until I get you home, Mrs. Holcomb, and I'll really surprise you. I think my hormones are telling me I need some very special attention."

"I can hardly wait," she giggled as she gave him a poke in his ribs.

It was soon the end of the dance, and Josh had dipped Liz to just the right angle so he could bend down and give her the kiss he had sworn he would get.

The whole place must have been watching as they all started clapping and laughing. Liz pulled away from him and ran to where Christy was standing. Her face was red and tears were running down her cheeks. "I want to go home right now, Christy. I can't face any of these people anymore tonight."

Jon walked over to where Josh was standing as Christy enveloped Liz in a hug and tried to console her quietly. "Liz, it's all right. Josh probably shouldn't have done that, but everyone was just enjoying the little love scene, not at all ridiculing. If you're going to spend time with him, it's going to require a lot of patience on your part because I see that Josh is a happy-go-lucky guy and does things on impulse. He is a very unpredictable, but wonderful brother-in-law, but he does take a bit of getting used to."

"Di-did you know I asked him to be my date at the Chri-Christmas Formal at school and he said he'd be hap-happy to?" she sobbed. "I wi-wish I hadn't asked him now, because huh-how do I know what he'll do that ni-night?" She'd gotten a tissue out of her pocket to wipe her eyes, and then she continued, "Christy, please don't let him take me home tonight without you and Jon. He was so cool this afternoon, helping me shop, and I was really so appreciative that without thinking where I was or what I was doing, I stood on my tiptoes and kissed him right there on the Main

Street sidewalk. Well, it was just on the cheek, but is his impulsiveness rubbing off on me? Wha-what am I go-going to do?" she hiccupped.

Christy couldn't help but smile. It sounded so much like what she'd gone through a few months ago when she was so unsure of her feelings for Jon and his intentions. *But, what kind of advice can I give her when she's still only sixteen years old, even though it won't be long until she's seventeen?* After a quick prayer, she whispered, "Liz, I'll give you the same advice Brent gave me when I was confused about trusting men and I almost turned Jon away. He told me to Trust God and obey my heart. It was very good advice, Liz."

"I'll try, Christy, but it seems useless when I'm so embarrassed right now."

Josh and Jon were standing a few feet away, and Josh had a very concerned look on his face. "Have I goofed it again, Jon? Liz has become rather important to me, but I'm not so sure it's possible for me to think about a real future with her. Maybe I should just try to find someone nearer my own age, when I get back to school, and let Liz get back to being a high school sophomore. I've promised to be her date for a Christmas Formal at her school, but that will be it, I'm afraid. Will you and Christy ride with us when I take her back to the ranch? I think she's ready to get away from me, for tonight at least."

"Sure, Josh. I'm sorry tonight ended the way it did, but I don't think you did anything wrong. It wasn't a long passionate kiss out there on the dance floor. It's just that she's a bit too young to handle the attention you got from the crowd."

"Yeah, my insistence and stubbornness to have my own way didn't help, either."

The ride to the ranch was a rather quiet one. Christy offered to ride in the back seat with Liz so Josh rode in front with Jon. Not a word was mentioned about the planned trip to the dealership the next morning. Josh jumped out and walked beside Liz to the door, tried to apologize for his behavior, but Liz wouldn't say a word as she escaped inside the house.

When Josh returned to the car, his throat was dry, his eyes wet, and all he wanted to do was try to get some sleep, but he feared it was going to be a long, sleepless night.

Chapter Ten

Saturday morning at 6:45 a.m. the phone started ringing beside Jon and Christy's bed. Sleepily, Jon asked, "Is it really time to get up?"

"Not quite," Christy replied and then a second later she laughed, "but it is now," as the alarm clock began beeping. "You'd better answer the phone."

"Oh, is that what that noise is?" Glancing quickly at the caller ID, he said "Hel-loo, is this an emergency or just a little prankster trying my patience by waking me up on a Saturday morning?"

"I'm so sorry, Jon. I thought you'd be up if you're still going to look for a truck, but I'll call back later."

"Hold on, Liz, it's OK," he chuckled. "The alarm went off about the same time the phone started to ring, so I'd be awake either way. You must've gotten up with the chickens, though. What can we do for you this morning?"

"I was almost afraid to call, but I wondered if I was still welcome to go with you guys this morning. I hate to miss out on the adventure to the dealership."

"Of course you're welcome. Why wouldn't you be? Do you think last night would change our minds about letting you go?"

"Maybe not yours or Christy's, but what about Josh?"

"Josh is fine, and he'll be thrilled that you still want to go. We'll pick you up just as we'd planned. I just checked the thermometer, though, and it's a little chilly outside. Do you have a warm jacket or should we bring one of Christy's for you? It's supposed to warm up so we may not need them for long, but I think something a little warmer will feel good to start out with, unless you're going to let Josh keep you warm."

"I think Josh would prefer to keep his distance from me. I brought my heavier jacket so I'll be fine. I don't know how to thank you, Jon, but just so I don't cause another problem, do you think Christy would mind sitting in the back seat with me?"

Jon couldn't keep from grinning as he said, "I'm sure she'll be happy to do that, Liz, but you're making too big a deal out of this. Josh is sorry he acted irrationally and hurt your feelings, but it wasn't enough to cause a big problem in your friendship, was it?"

"I guess not. I just don't know how to react to some of his teasing and mischievous stunts. I'll be ready when you get here, though, because I'm not going to let him make me miss out on this fun adventure."

"That's the spirit. Be sure to eat some breakfast, and we'll pick you up around 8:30. Bye for now."

By the time Jon had dressed and gotten to the kitchen, Josh had arrived at their door wanting to know if they were going to eat breakfast here or on the road. Christy motioned for him to come in and pointed to the grill where there were pancakes, bacon, and eggs sizzling. The smell of the bacon, plus the coffee brewing, made his mouth water.

"How do you ladies do all this? Mom seems to know just when to have food ready, and you're just the same. I guess that's why I love the ladies so much although there are a few who don't love me back." His quick grin was as captivating as Jon's, and Christy gave him a little kiss on the cheek, but she couldn't miss the return of a rather solemn expression.

"We love cooking for hungry, appreciative men, and you're right on time for a warm and filling breakfast on a rather cool morning, Josh, so grab a plate and help yourself. It's going to be a great day! Jon finally got here so you can eat together, but maybe one of you could pour the orange juice."

"I'll do that and then we'd better start eating so we can get on our way," Jon added. "It feels chilly this morning, but the forecast is for sunny skies and warming into the 60's so riding this afternoon should be great if things work out for buying a truck. I'm really looking forward to checking out all he has available because I think I'm as excited as Liz. This is a new experience for me, too."

"You could always get excited when something new was being planned, but it won't be much fun for me today if Liz refuses to go along." Josh looked so sad that Jon decided to assure him that Liz called and still wanted to go with them. "She did ask if Christy would sit in the back seat with her, however."

"Just as long as she's with us, that's OK. Maybe I can work a miracle with my little princess." That brought the grin back and his breakfast disappeared. "Just another cup of coffee and I'll be ready."

Liz was waiting when they arrived at the ranch at exactly 8:30. She looked a little sheepishly at the guys and then climbed in the back seat beside Christy. "Tell me the truth, am I in the doghouse?" she whispered in Christy's ear.

Christy just shook her head and whispered back,

"Just forget it, Liz, please. It was no catastrophe. You should've seen the grin return to Josh's face when Jon told him you'd called and still wanted to go."

"You're just trying to make me feel better, aren't you? I'm not going to say a word today and then I won't cause another problem."

"That might create a bigger problem. Please, just be yourself."

"Did I hear something about a problem from the back seat?" Jon asked as he was looking at them in the rearview mirror. "There are going to be no problems today. We're going to buy a truck for Dad, we're going to go riding this afternoon, and then maybe we can get to that movie we missed last night. Or, if you wish, we'll try our hand at playing some board game like Monopoly or Scrabble. How does that sound?"

"I would prefer going to the movie after riding, if my preference counts," Josh said very softly and a little hesitantly. "I'd like a soft seat, a warm room, some popcorn and a drink, and hopefully, a cute little sixteen-year-old by my side. Since this will probably be the last night we'll be together for awhile, could we spend it doing something relaxing and fun?" He turned part-way around, looked at Liz, smiled and asked, "Pretty please?"

Liz was blushing as she looked at him and then at Christy. "How do you say 'No' to these guys? I really would like to see that new movie that's playing, but I'll go along with whatever the rest of you decide. I'm just so happy to be doing something different and very exciting."

The day progressed well. When Fred saw Christy, he elected to personally show them his inventory of what they were interested in. He pointed out eight small trucks and opened the hood of each one so they could see that the engines were very clean, (what did any of the four know about engines, anyway). Fred told them the type of tires mounted on each, and also the previous owner/owners. He checked the mileage for them, and then also started each one so they could hear the engine running.

They all seemed to be drawn to a three-year-old red Dodge Ram and decided to take it for a test drive. Of course, they all wanted to go, and Fred chuckled as all four of them tried to get on the single bench seat to no avail. Liz and Christy finally stayed behind while Jon and Josh checked it out. They were really pleased with the way it handled, sounded, and looked so they went inside to do the paper work, which also went very smoothly. By 11:30 everything was in order and they were ready to visit the restaurant just across the road.

Josh walked over to Liz and asked, "Would you possibly consider riding with me in the little red Ram?

I'll be on my best behavior today, Liz, if you'll give me a chance."

She hesitated, glanced at Christy who smiled and nodded, and then turned back to Josh and said, "I'd love to ride in the little red Ram, Mr. Holcomb, but do you really know how to drive it? I'd hate ending up in a ditch somewhere."

"Mr. Holcomb is still my father and I'm just Josh," he grinned, "but I do know how to drive a truck and I'll be extra careful with a princess by my side." Turning toward the others, he asked, "Are we ready to eat lunch?"

"You know your brother too well to ask that question, Josh," Christy chuckled as she grabbed Jon's arm and headed for the Tahoe. "We'll see you across the road."

∽

As predicted, the sun had shown all morning and the weather was perfect for riding by early afternoon. When Marge and Rachel learned they were going riding and then to a movie, they asked if they'd join them for an early supper. Jon and Josh were delighted, of course.

Brent was in the barn when the four arrived to get the horses saddled for their ride. He ambled over to ask Jon and Josh if they would mind riding a couple of the horses that hadn't been on the trails for awhile.

"Just so mine isn't easily spooked," Josh laughed.

"These two, Black Beard and Ramrod, are a little older, 4 years old to be exact, but they know the trails real well. It's just that lately all the riders seem to be asking for the yearlings."

"My horse, Moonlight, is 5 years old, and Jon usually rides My Spirit who is almost 7, so we should get along well with Black Beard and Ramrod," Josh remarked as Brent led the way to the stalls.

Christy and Liz had Rainbow and Starbright saddled and ready to go when the guys joined them. They followed the regular trail for half an hour before Christy turned off to head toward the mountains. She led them into a grove of mostly evergreens that were lush and green, but they immediately wished they'd worn the heavier coats instead of changing into the lighter ones. "This is where we usually ride during the hot summer days," Christy explained, "because it's normally at least 20 degrees cooler. I won't keep you in here very long today."

Coming into the sunshine again was a welcomed relief and they continued on up the mountain incline. Making a turn to the south, they soon came to a large mountain lake with at least four cabins scattered here and there. "Ours is the closest cabin," Christy explained, but she had pulled up and was just surveying the lake and spectacular beauty. "We should come up here more often to enjoy the view, but our cabin wasn't built for convenience." she chuckled.

"It was still lots of fun to come and hide out for a few hours," Liz added. "Shall we see what condition it was left in?"

"If you want to, Liz, but I'm going to sit here on this log right now and drink in the gorgeous surroundings." She dismounted and led Rainbow to the water's edge and then sat down on a good-sized log near by that had been cut and sanded smooth for a great bench.

They all joined her as she had pulled a thermos of hot cocoa and four cups from her saddlebag. Liz had a bunch of cookies that her mother had given her as they were leaving the house, so they sat there and enjoyed a tasty snack.

They decided to take a quick tour of the cabin then, and the girls were surprised to find that a lot of updating had been done since they'd been here last. "Wow, this is really a nice little cabin now," Christy almost whispered as she went around the sitting room and kitchen. She went to peek into the two bedrooms with Liz close behind.

"I can't believe it's the same place," Liz said as she opened another door. "Oh, they even put in a bathroom, Christy. Remember the outdoor one we had to use with the spiders and bad smell?" she giggled as she wrinkled up her nose. "I always hated to even think about going out there."

"It's too bad we don't have time to build a fire in the fireplace today. Maybe we'll have to make another trip out here before the winter snow prohibits it." Christy caught Jon watching her and grinning. "Oh, what a lovely rendezvous spot," she murmured.

Josh had seen their exchanged glances and felt a tug in his chest informing him that he would love to have what Jon is experiencing. *I know it's not quite time for me, however,* he silently reminded himself. *I have things to get completed first, just as Jon did when he was my age. I've got to let God open the doors, and if Liz is to be in my future, it will just happen in His time.*

The ride back was pretty direct, and they arrived in plenty of time to get the horses stalled and to freshen up a bit before dinner. Brad, Brent, and Susan were there, and when asked if they wanted to go with them to the movie, they all agreed. With the early supper over and the dishes done, they headed to town in two cars.

Josh wasn't quite sure how to behave with Liz sitting so quietly beside him and her brother, Brad, sitting on the other side of her. She was eating her popcorn and had her eyes glued to the screen. Then, at one point, she just reached over and took his hand, looked up at him, and whispered, "Thank you, Josh, for not holding it against me for being so young and sensitive."

"You'll always be my sweet mysterious princess, and I could never hold it against you for being sensitive when a jerk embarrasses you," he whispered back. He leaned over and kissed the top of her head and continued holding her hand. *I'm always so content when I'm with her, but also so aware of what I said to Jon last night. I still feel strongly that I should let her enjoy her high school years. But, can I actually do it?*

As much as he wanted to drive her back to the ranch, Liz decided that she should ride with Brad, Brent and Susan. He had to settle for the fact that he would see her once again at church tomorrow, before he'd probably head home going south while Liz, with her mother and Brad, would drive north to Colorado Springs. He fought back tears that were trying to well up in his eyes as he said, "Goodnight, Princess," but he was a little surprised to see her wiping her eyes as she walked beside her brother toward Brent's car.

Chapter Eleven

The worship service was quite interesting to Josh today because he'd decided to listen much closer to what the pastors were saying. Since he'd seen the accident when the baby had been thrown from the child's car seat and down the ravine and was still found unharmed, he'd realized he had seen a miracle with his own eyes. He felt God was definitely trying to tell him something and he was ready to listen, especially when one of the scripture verses today was Psalm 46:10; "Be still, and know that I am God!"

Jon and Christy were singing in the choir so he sat with Liz and her family. He had to admit that his mind wandered a little as he couldn't keep from glancing at her and wanting to touch her soft blonde hair she had pulled back in a pony tail this morning.

He just wished they didn't have to part. She looked over at him, smiled that beautiful smile that he loves to see, and then she took his hand in hers to hold the rest of the service.

Afterwards, they were all going to the ranch for lunch and asked if he would like to join them. He thought he had better get started toward home, so they exchanged farewells in the church parking lot. He got a chance to talk to Liz for just a moment. He whispered, "I'll be talking to you real soon, Princess. Remember, I'm definitely planning to take you to your Christmas prom, so don't go home and ask one of those nerds, you hear?"

She smiled and whispered back, "I'm looking forward to it, Josh, and I'll never be able to thank you enough for all you've done for me." She reached out her arms for a hug, and, of course, he took that opportunity to hold her rather snugly and kiss her forehead.

After a quick hug and a thank you for Jon and Christy, Josh almost ran to the truck that he'd driven to the church. He took off before anyone could see the tears welling up in his eyes again. He stopped at the little diner across from the dealership, where they'd eaten yesterday, but that, too, just brought back memories and he ate very little. *If this is how it feels to be in love, I'm not at all sure it's really worth it, but I wouldn't want to change the feelings I have for my little princess, either.* "Dear God, could you give me just a hint of what your plans are for me?" he prayed aloud as he drove toward home.

Jon had given him good directions to Lamar, and then he was familiar with the road on home. It was a rather melancholy drive as he couldn't get his mind off Liz, but it made the time go by a little faster. He was home before dark and in time for his mother's great cooking. His dad was glad to see him, too, because Janice wasn't feeling well, Matthew had gone out of town with his family, so he could certainly use his help finishing the chores.

⌁

Liz, with her mother and Brad, started home shortly after lunch. Liz elected to sit in the back seat, which surprised Brad because she usually insisted on sitting in the front with their mother. "Are you all right?" he asked as she climbed in.

"I'm okay, but I think I may curl up and take a little nap on the way home. It's been a rather busy weekend."

"I guess. With everyone becoming couples down here, I'm going to have to find a girl of my own or stay home with my head stuck in a book," he pouted.

Liz grabbed one of the pillows they had in the van and curled up on the back seat, but she couldn't fall asleep. *How can just one very irritating guy, one who likes to humiliate and tease me, but then be one of the sweetest guys on earth, have such a hold on my life or heart?*

Of course, she had no answer so she softly prayed. "Dear Jesus, please hear my plea. I'm so confused. Josh still seems to mean so much to me when our ages, our schooling, and even the distance between us are such problems. I can't even imagine that he would consider waiting two more years for me to just finish high school after he graduates this spring from college. I'd never even cared about boys until I met Josh, but then he keeps upsetting me with his spontaneous pranks. I'd really like to hate him, but I can't because he has that cool charm about him. As soon as we have to say goodbye, I'm ready to cry, and I think he is, too. Does that mean something, Dear Jesus? Can your plans really include the two of us being together someday? You know I've put my life in your hands, but does it have to be so perplexed?"

She quickly sat up in the seat when some verses from Proverbs 3 came to her. She had learned them when a wonderful missionary couple had been at their church for a series of youth meetings. One of them would be drawing a picture depicting the theme of the story as the other was telling it. They'd always taught a scripture verse or verses each evening, too. One was 'Trust in the Lord with all your heart and lean not on your own understanding; in all your ways acknowledge Him, and He will make your paths straight.' She'd learned the few following verses, also, which said, 'Do not be wise in your own eyes, but fear the Lord and shun evil. This will bring health to your body and nourishment to your bones.'

"What an immediate answer to my prayer, Dear Lord. Thank You," she whispered. She put her head back on the pillow and soon fell asleep. Her dad's voice woke her as he'd come out of the house to help carry in the luggage.

"Well, I see we have a sleeping beauty in the car today. Did they truly run the fairy princess ragged with all the activities your mom told me about?"

"It was an exciting weekend, Dad. Those three, Jon, Christy, and Josh can really keep things hopping. I'll have to give you some details later." She gave him a hug and then hurried inside.

⁙

The next three weeks went by quickly for Liz as the teachers seemed to be pouring on homework before Christmas vacation. She was cramming for tests almost every night, but she felt she had done well on all of them. Josh had called a couple of times, and now the day of the dance had arrived. Classes were dismissed, after a short assembly following lunch, and she was elated because she could relax for awhile and still have plenty of time to be ready before Mr. Know-It-All arrives. *He's so sure he's going to have to wait for me to finish dressing, but I'm going to be tapping my toes and waiting for him to show up.*

She went to her room and stretched out on her bed. She hadn't meant to, but she let her eyes close and was soon asleep. When her mother came to check on her, it was almost 5 o'clock. Josh would be there at 6:30 because he'd asked to take her to dinner before going to the dance. She was frantic. She raced to the shower, her hair was tangled from her sleeping, and her eyes were red and a little puffy. What was she going to do? Luckily, the shower calmed her a little, some drops in her eyes cleared the red out, and Mary came in just long enough to help with her make-up and her hair. She had everything else on and was now ready for her dress.

She glanced at the clock and then screamed as she realized it was 6:20. She rushed to the closet and got her dress, but then she realized she needed someone to zip it up the back. Mary had already gone downstairs, now the doorbell was ringing, and she was as nervous as an actor on opening night. Who was going to help her? She heard footsteps on the stairs and ran to the door. She saw her dad coming up the steps. "Josh is here," he announced as she grabbed his hand and pulled him into her room.

"Dad, please, I can't get into this dress without someone to zip it up the back. Can you do that for me?"

Chuckling, he closed the door behind him and turned her around so he could see the back of the dress. "I think I've done this a few times before tonight, but I thought you were going to be ready early so Josh wouldn't have to wait for you. Did you forget to set your alarm before you decided to take a little beauty nap? It appears that you're going to be a bit later than his five minutes at the ranch now."

"Oh, hush, Dad. I didn't mean to go to sleep, and I'm going to get enough ribbing from Josh without you helping him out with those reminders. Are you about done?"

"Well, I'm having a little problem. The zipper has gotten caught in the material of the dress and I'm afraid I'll tear it. I'm going to have to get your mother, if she's back from her errand to the cleaners. Apparently she forgot to pick up the coat Mary wants to wear to the dance tonight. Luckily, Damon isn't picking her up quite so early. I'll be right back."

Liz was pacing the floor when the door opened again and she looked into the eyes of Josh standing there with her father. "What is he doing up here?" she asked, almost in tears.

"I thought I'd better tell him what the problem

was, Sweetheart, and he might not be so hard on you if he knew it was my fault, in a way. He assured me that he could help with the situation, so I brought him up. Now, turn around so he can see what he can do."

"Dad, my dress is unzipped. Josh shouldn't see me this way."

Josh had slipped around her, while she was arguing with her dad, and had quickly seen the problem. He put his mouth close to her ear to whisper that he would have it fixed in just a second when she whirled around and their lips met perfectly. She jumped back, red faced and teary eyed, wandering what her dad was going to say about that, but then she heard him laughing.

"Liz, please turn around and let Josh see if he can fix your zipper or you'll never get to the dance. I'm sorry I messed it up, but let's get this show on the road." She reluctantly turned around, but then decided that was better than having to look into his beautiful brown eyes that were sure to be teasing. He must've had a lot of experience with zippers, though, because he had it fixed in seconds.

"There you are, Princess, all fixed and zipped up. I didn't see a thing that I haven't seen on Janice many times when I had to zip her up." He glanced over at Dr. Becker and couldn't miss his amused smile.

❧

They were soon on their way, and Josh had decided that not a word was going to be said about her being late. It appeared that she had punished herself enough, and he didn't want to add to it.

He had picked a chain restaurant that he knew served excellent food near campus, so they went there and he wasn't disappointed. When he'd made the reservation, he'd asked for a corner booth that would be a little more private, and they'd held it for him. He'd been so pleased when she had made a fuss over the wrist corsage of yellow roses that he'd gotten her, and now he had another gift he wanted her to have. After they had placed their order, he scooted out of his side of the booth and slid in beside her.

"What are you doing now, Josh? You're not going to embarrass me again tonight, are you, by kissing me right here in the restaurant?"

"As much as I'd love to kiss you, that's not what I have in mind, right now anyway." He was grinning as he pulled out a narrow jewelry box, about 3" long, from his coat pocket. "This gift, Princess, is something I hope you'll wear and maybe remember me now and then." He just happened to glance around and saw the waitress heading their way, so he whispered, "This was very poor timing because our drinks are coming. Maybe we'll wait and you can open it later." He scooted back to his side of the booth.

The dance was a typical high school affair with most of the girls on one side of the gym floor and the boys on the other.

The dance was a typical high school affair with most of the girls on one side of the gym floor and the boys on the other. The guys were all dressed well in suits or even a tux, and the girls looked like a page from the latest fashion magazine, but it was as if a barbed wire fence separated them. They looked, they saw, but somehow they couldn't touch. "I'd thought this was a formal dance for couples," Josh remarked after they had finished a rather jumpy tune. "This could pass for any old Friday night dance at the youth center. You had me wear this...ah, nothing; I'm thrilled to be here with you."

"I told you the guys at this school are a bunch of nerds. The girls just give up and come as a group, dance together unless a guy gets up enough nerve to ask one of them to dance, and then the girls usually go to one of the homes for an overnight. It's really crazy. That's why I wouldn't have come if I hadn't had a date. Oh, there's Mary and Damon. They make a cute couple, don't they?"

"Yeah, but not as cute as we are," he chuckled. Putting his arm around her, he then pulled her toward him and kissed the top of her head. She was such a petite thing, but he knew she wouldn't break, the way she played tennis and rode those horses.

Like at the wedding reception, she was still reluctant to dance cheek to cheek, but by the end of the evening he thought he had made a little progress. He'd noticed some of the guys watching them as they were dancing and he'd tried to give them a gentle hint with a head motion. After a while, a few had finally sidled over and asked some of the girls to dance. There were, actually, quite a few couples who appeared to be on dates, but the singles certainly outnumbered them.

They finally met up with Mary and Damon for some refreshments. Parents had been asked to furnish cookies, brownies, small sandwiches and chips, but after their earlier dinner, they decided just to share a can of soda. Mary and Damon had a sandwich and a brownie and then went back to the dance floor. Josh and Liz lingered over their drink and enjoyed watching the dancing styles of the different couples.

"We probably shouldn't stay too late if you have to drive--oh, Josh, I forgot to ask you where you were going to stay tonight. I'm sorry; we could've had you stay with us."

"No, that wouldn't have been right, but I'm not driving back tonight, even to Hayes. I reserved a room here so I can be rested and alert. I usually prefer to drive during the day, especially on the weekend."

"Will you leave early in the morning then or will you stay with Jon and Christy tomorrow night and drive home Sunday?"

"You're a curious little one, aren't you, Princess?

Is there something going on in that little head of yours that I might like to know about? Like, would I pick you up and take you for breakfast before I leave? Would you be willing to do that and maybe show me around your hometown a bit?"

"I'd love that, Josh. Why don't we dance one more time and then leave. It's after 11 o'clock now and the dance ends at 11:30. The school is hoping everyone will be home by midnight, but I don't imagine many make it by then."

He took her in his arms for a slow dance that was just beginning, and to his surprise, she snuggled up close to him and put her head against his shoulder. He realized that she'd have to be on her tiptoes, or be wearing very high heels, to actually dance cheek to cheek with him. He tried to remember how it had been when they'd danced at the Pub and Grub, but he could only remember the one dance when he'd kissed her. He'd been holding her so tight, to keep her from squirming, maybe he'd had her feet off the floor. He smiled as his chin rested on the top of her head and she seemed content to be held close to him tonight.

◈

He'd seen a small park on the way to the school so now he pulled in and parked. Of course, he saw the fright on her face and chuckled. "Liz, I'm not going to try anything. If you remember, I mentioned at the restaurant that maybe you could open the present I have for you later. Well, this is later and here is the present. Let's see if you like it."

As he watched her beautiful eyes reflecting the delight of a gift, she daintily took the ribbon from around the box and then looked inside. Her eyes lit up like diamonds when she saw the locket, but when she opened it and saw a tiny picture of him, she gasped. "Oh, Josh, I'm so thrilled. I'll have you near me all the time now because I'll never take it off, except to shower, I guess." She turned so she could stretch her arms over to him, put them up around his neck and pull him closer to her. He had never realized that a tiny sixteen-year-old could kiss like that. Well, almost seventeen, but even so, he was astounded. He couldn't remember ever getting a kiss that had given him so many tingles, and he'd had his share of kisses over the years.

"I'd better get you home now," he moaned.

"Oh, Josh, I don't want to go home. I'm having all these feelings that I don't really understand, but I don't want to leave you."

"Princess, have you had a talk with your mom about dating?"

"Yes, Josh, I have," she giggled. "Are the things she was trying to explain to me what I'm feeling tonight?"

"Most likely, and that's why I need to get you home. My feelings aren't quite dead or in control tonight either."

"Oh, I'm sorry, Josh, but I'm so glad it's you I'm with tonight. You've always been so patient with me. I've usually felt so safe with you, but if you're not in control tonight, I guess you'd better take me home now. I'm glad to know what I need to watch out for, though. She patted his cheek, then sat back to admire the locket and whisper, "My hero and my love."

Chapter Twelve

Liz awoke Saturday morning all dreamy eyed and smiling. She reached up to her throat to touch the locket Josh had given her the night before. As she remembers his words, however, that he hoped she would wear it and remember him now and then, she starts to cry.

He's going to tell me he doesn't want to see me anymore! I felt so close to him last night, I actually thought he was going to be the one I'd share my life with, but I guess it isn't in God's plan if that is what Josh is going to do. I'll just have to be brave and strong and try to get through this morning with him without crying or making a fool of myself. She then crawled out of bed, showered and put on her clothes although her heart was no longer in it.

Her mother appeared at the door about 7 o'clock and asked if she was going to eat some breakfast. Liz just shook her head. "Josh is going to take me to breakfast before he goes back to Hayes, but from something he said last night, I think he's going to tell me he doesn't want to see me anymore. I've really had so much fun with him, Mom, and I've also learned a lot about the feelings a person has when she begins to think of someone as more than a friend," she giggled. "It confirmed our little talks but with more clarity than just a few words. Although he certainly infuriated me at times, and I *am* aware that our ages are a concern to all of us, he has been so patient with me, sort of like a teacher and a protector."

"I'm certainly glad to hear that, Sweetie. Your dad and I have certainly had some concerns about the age difference. We could only pray that your morals and training would keep you safe as well as Josh being the person he appeared to be."

"He just kept reminding me that I have my high school years to enjoy, and he doesn't want to keep me from enjoying them to the fullest. What do I say to him, Mom?"

"This is one of the hardest times of your life, Liz, losing your first love, if that is what you feel this has been. I think Josh is being very wise to let you finish your high school years without a commitment to him or anyone else. If this relationship is meant to be, God will see that the two of you get back together when the time is right. As to what to say to him, I'd suggest that you say what is in your heart. Be truthful and he'll admire you for it. You know that you'll probably see him at the ranch occasionally, when he comes to see Jon and Christy, so you'll want to stay friends. That way, you won't be losing contact with him completely."

"Thanks, Mom, that's a good thought. I just hope I can make it easy for both of us by suggesting we continue to share an e-mail or phone call occasionally, and when we see each other at the ranch, we can enjoy the time as friends or rivals, especially on the tennis court." She smiled mischievously as she saw her reflection in the mirror while combing her hair.

"If he's going to pick you up this morning, I'd better scoot so you can finish dressing and be ready on time." Smiling, she said, "I'm really sorry I wasn't here to help with your zipper last night, but I guess Josh must be an expert in that area. Have you tried using Brad's expertise along those lines?" She couldn't keep from laughing as she added, "I don't think I'd try that any time soon, if I were you."

❧

At 7:50 Liz was at the front window watching for Josh to pull into the drive. *Well,* she thought rather disappointedly, *at least I'm ready and my coat is right here beside me, so he won't get the chance to tease me about being late this time. Come to think of it, he didn't even mention my being late last night. That's rather surprising, but endearing, which makes it all the harder to say goodbye.* When the grandfather clock started to chime the hour, she became a little concerned. *He said he'd see me at 8 o'clock, so where is he?*

Josh was circling several blocks, watching the minutes go by, because he was trying to deliberately be late. He didn't want his Princess thinking he was always so punctual that he would never allow her to have a few extra minutes without getting teased. So, at 8:08 he pulled into the drive, his heart beating overtime because he wasn't anxious to do what he felt he had to do this morning. He jumped out of the Tahoe and headed for the door.

When he saw Liz looking out the window, his heart was in his throat, but this was something he felt God wanted him to do, and maybe they both needed time to discover if their friendship was just that, a very close friendship, or if it could, someday, develop into something that could last a lifetime.

Liz, of course, saw him pull in and she had to force back the tears as she realized just how hard it was going to be to let him go. He looked so handsome in his jeans and the nice flannel shirt she could see beneath his open denim jacket. His athletic build, brown hair and eyes were so much like Jon that she wondered if she would have to avoid Jon now when they went to the ranch. *Will I ever be able to forget how it felt dancing with Josh last night with his arms around me and my head against his shoulder?* Her musings were soon interrupted by the doorbell, and she scurried to meet him with her coat and purse in her hands.

"Good morning, Princess, I'm sorry I'm a little late again. Do you want to scold me or are we ready to go? I'm getting pretty hungry--how about you?"

"My appetite has somewhat disappeared this morning, but I'll try to eat something. It's been rather hard to keep my thoughts from running a little wild. When I see the menu, maybe I'll find something that looks good to me."

He put his arm across her shoulders on the way to the car, helped her in and hurried around to the driver's seat. "I'm sorry, Darlin', didn't you sleep well? I thought you looked pretty tired after the dance, and I hoped you could dream of me holding you, dancing with you, and maybe even reliving the kiss you gave me after opening the gift. Man, did I ever enjoy that," he chuckled. He slid his hand across the seat, picked up her left hand and then brought her fingers to his lips. He kissed each one but then dropped her hand suddenly as he remembered what he had to do this morning. *Don't make it any harder than it already is,* he silently scolded himself.

He backed out of the drive and headed toward an IHOP restaurant that he'd spotted on his way to her house. He'd decided that would be a good place to eat and, hopefully, a quiet place to talk. After pulling into a parking space, he raced around to open the door for her so she wouldn't get out on her own. His hands were around her waist as he lifted her down, but it was so hard not to pull her into his arms for a kiss. She smiled, but he could see the little blush in her cheeks. He loved her youthful innocence, and it was tearing him apart that he felt he had to walk away.

When they had placed their order, he didn't know whether to wait until they'd eaten or to just go ahead and get it over with. She'd actually ordered a pretty good breakfast, and he wanted her to enjoy her food. He'd decided to wait until later to talk about the future, but for some reason, he then couldn't think of a single thing to say. He could only sit and look at her or stare out the window. He felt like an absolute fool.

It was Liz who finally started the conversation. "Josh, when I woke up this morning and reached up to touch my beautiful locket, I remembered what you had said last night at the restaurant when you started to give me the gift. You said that you hoped I would wear it and remember you now and then. It didn't register then, but it certainly did this morning.

Now you are trying so hard to get up the courage to tell me exactly what you meant, aren't you, without it hurting me too deeply? However, it's upsetting you more each minute you try to put it off. I think I understand why you've decided to stop seeing me, Josh, and I admire you for it. Maybe, someday, I'll even be able to agree that my high school days were happy, exciting times, and possibly even necessary; but right now I wish I were a 1000 miles away from that school.

I think I told you that I've put my life in God's hands, and I accept this step as a part of His plan. Wherever He leads me, I plan to follow, but if someday that leads back to you, I'll be thrilled. My only request is that we try to remain friends, maybe share an e-mail or a phone call once in a while, just to keep in touch. I also hope we'll be able to actually tolerate each other when we're both at the ranch." She forced a giggle and then asked, "Did that help you a little with your own speech?"

Her smile gave him the courage to speak. "The Mysterious Princess is certainly the right name for you, Liz. You're really awesome, do you know that? I'm so afraid you can read me as easily as you do a book. I just wish the situation was such that I could ask you to marry me right now so I could love, adore, and worship you the rest of my life, but I know that isn't the answer. It wouldn't be right for you or right in God's eyes. I happened to open the Bible at the motel this morning to Ephesians 6:11 which said 'Put on the full armor of God so that you can take your stand against all the devil's schemes.' Liz, I truly intend to do that and I hope to grow to be as strong in my faith as you are in yours. In fact, I've decided to sign up for a class on the study of the Bible during the next semester and see what I can discover that I missed during my rebellious years."

"Well, it looks like we got all that out of the way just in time, Josh." After the server had placed their plates in front of them, she continued, "Now we can just enjoy our breakfast without anything hanging over our heads. My food really looks good, and yours does, too." Their conversation was rather light, however, except for a few smiles, as they ate.

She took him on a rather short tour of the city, but it included the front of the school he couldn't see very well in the dark last night, and also the front of the hospital where her dad has his office and, of course, where Josh had recovered from the concussion. She also pointed out some of the bigger stores he wasn't familiar with. He'd told her that growing up in the little town in Oklahoma hadn't given him that opportunity and also explained that most of their vacations had been to lake resorts rather than to large cities because his mother was very nervous and insecure in populous places. The zoo and a couple museums were also included on the tour, and then she wanted to show him the club house and part of the golf course in the development where their home is located. When she'd finished doing that, she then sat back on the seat and tried to get prepared for his goodbye as she'd assumed that he would now be taking her home.

However, he drove back to the little park where they had stopped after the dance for her to open the present. He turned off the engine and took a deep breath. As he turned to look at her, he tried to give her one of his reassuring smiles, but he certainly didn't feel like everything was so hunky-dory. "Liz, can we just talk for a little while before I have to take you home?"

"Of course, Josh. Is there something special you want to talk about?" She heard her voice waver just a bit, but she forced a smile to try to calm both of their emotions.

"No. It's just that I don't want to leave quite yet. Maybe we could talk about family Christmas plans. Do you go to the ranch for Christmas or do you celebrate at home?"

"We stay home for Christmas. That has always been our tradition, and I've always loved the low key family setting. The fireplace is blazing, and we open the gifts one at a time so we see each present and the expression on the face of the one receiving it. It's so much fun to see the look on a person's face if he or she isn't especially happy with the gift. Will your family plans change this year with Jon married?"

"It'll be different, that's for sure."

"Do you know what Jon and Christy are going to do yet?"

"Jon and Christy are spending Christmas Day at the ranch, and then they're planning to come down and spend the week with us, so I imagine our Christmas will be put off until they get there. Our gift opening has always been quite similar to yours. I don't think our four grandparents have ever missed coming to spend Christmas Eve and staying the night so they don't miss anything. When we were little, they always seemed more excited than us kids on Christmas morning."

"That sounds so cool. I'm told that my dad's parents were killed in an automobile accident when I was just four years old, so I don't remember them very well. I have always remembered a Santa Claus coming to our door one Christmas Eve, though, and I had been so thrilled. It was the Christmas I got my large tricycle and a special doll I'd asked for, but I wasn't told until much later that it had been Grandpa Becker playing Santa."

"What a wonderful memory to have, though, instead of an accident. Do you know what kind of plans are in the works for your birthday? Since it's on a Tuesday, I guess I'll have to let someone else be the first to kiss you after you turn seventeen. Not that you'd consider inviting me now, anyway. Could I possibly hold the honor of being the last to kiss you *before* your birthday, though? Just between you and me, that is?"

"Oh, that's quite an honor, Josh, but you'll probably be able to keep that one. I'm not anticipating a kiss from anyone else unless it's family. As far as any plans, I wanted to have something at the ranch, but Dad thinks I should invite some of my friends from school and have a reception of some kind at the club. I asked if we could do it on the weekend, but he insists that it be on the exact day, and so it'll have to be on Tuesday, February 14th, because when my dad speaks, everyone listens," she implied with as deep a voice as she could.

"That sounds like a good plan to me, Princess. I'm just sorry I won't be able to be there to meet your friends and see the rest of the family. Maybe your dad feels your trip to Spain will be part of your celebration. Will you be going to a certain city in Spain?"

"I guess I haven't told you about that! The trip is to Barcelona, and Dad and Mom have mentioned, *if* I am chosen to go on the trip, they might plan a trip to Paris about that time. When the week is over in Barcelona, I could join them for a few days in Paris and be able to practice my French, too. Isn't that cool? I'd miss a few days of school, but that would be OK."

"Wow, I guess you do have a great spring break to look forward to. Will Mary and Brad get to travel, too?"

"From what I've heard, Mary wants to go with a chaperoned group on a trip to San Francisco. I don't think Brad's break is at the same time as ours, so he'll probably be in school. He hasn't mentioned any plans that I know of."

"I guess time is slipping away, Princess, so do you think I should take you home and get on my way? You did ask about my travel plans last night but I guess I didn't tell you. You pretty well guessed it, though, that I'll spend tonight in Hayes and then drive on home tomorrow after church. I sure wish you were going to be there to sit beside me. I'm sorry, Liz, I just can't believe that I'm going to shelve what we've come to mean to each other, or at least what you mean to me, but I'm also pretty sure this is the right thing to do. I do hope we can keep in touch, remain friends like you mentioned, and see each other occasionally at the ranch. We'd better get you home now before I change my mind and kidnap you. I can just imagine how that would upset a few folks." He reached over and pulled her to him. "Could I have just one more of those kisses, please, before I have to become a recluse?"

She quickly turned toward him, reached her arms around his neck and gave him a kiss she hoped he'd remember for a long, long time. At this particular moment, she never wanted him to forget her.

"Oh, Princess, how do you expect me to live a lonely, solitary life knowing there are kisses as sweet as that one waiting for me?"

They both were laughing as he started the engine, but when he shifted into gear, he realized that a police car had just pulled up behind him. "Oh, no, I guess we stayed here a couple of minutes too long. He's writing my license number down." He turned the engine off and waited with a little anxiety to find out what he had done wrong.

"Hello, Officer. My friend and I were saying our goodbyes and I was just heading to her house to drop her off. Is there anything wrong?"

"No, I guess not with the two of you," he said as he'd stooped down to look in the window. "Hello, Liz. I assume you know this young man from Oklahoma and feel you're safe with him?"

"Oh, yes, Calvin. You were on duty and couldn't

attend Christy's wedding back in October, but this is Josh Holcomb whose brother married Christy. He came to be my escort to the Christmas dance last night and then took me to breakfast this morning. He's going to drive to Hayes as soon as he drops me off at home, and then he'll drive on to Oklahoma on Sunday. Josh, this is my cousin, Calvin Becker." After the two men had exchanged their greetings and shaken hands, Liz then asked, "Is there someone special you're looking for?"

"Yeah, we've had a kidnapping and the suspect is driving an out-of-state truck."

"So that's why you're checking Josh's Tahoe?"

"Since some people refer to a Tahoe as a truck, I thought I'd better check this one out. I'm glad I could eliminate you, Josh, without any trouble."

"Well, I hope you catch the one you're looking for before he gets out of the area, if he has someone against their will," Josh remarked.

"Thanks, and have a good day, both of you. Liz, tell your family hello for me." He quickly returned to the squad car and was on his way.

"Whew, that was a little scary and also quite a coincidence so soon after my talking about kidnapping you, huh? I hope I can get out of the city without being stopped again, but I didn't know you had a cousin who was a police officer."

"He's been on the force for about four years, but

139

I think you'll be OK. You have such an honest face," she giggled.

"Thanks for nothing, Liz. I guess it's certainly time to take you home before we get into any more unusual circumstances."

"I guess we *have* had our share of unusual things happen when we've been together, haven't we? They started the very first day we met, too. What do you suppose that means, Josh? Is it an omen or was it just the way God planned it so we could really get to know each other."

"Do you think we really know each other, Liz?" You can read my mind, that's for sure, but I'm always in awe of you and your extraordinary talents. Maybe you came along just to make sure I saw God in a true light."

"If I did that, Josh, I'm so pleased. I know it'll make a big difference in your life."

"It's just too bad we don't live closer to each other so we could learn more about God together, but maybe we can do some of that in our e-mails; if you still want to keep in touch with me, that is. It's been fun since the wedding, but you may not want to continue now that I'm sort of stepping out of your life."

"I think we should remain in touch if only for the family's sake. After all, we *are* sort of related now, and you can't walk away completely," she giggled.

"I guess you're right, so can I continue to call you on the phone once in a while, too, to catch up on how you're doing?"

"I'd love that, Josh."

As he started the engine, his eyes were soaking in all the beauty they could of this one mysterious princess who had come into his life. He could only hope that this wasn't the end of their friendship or maybe even a very meaningful relationship in the future.

Chapter Thirteen

Jon took one look at Josh, when he arrived at their apartment in Hayes, and knew that his brother was hurting and definitely needed a heart to heart talk. He quickly glanced over at Christy, and she nodded as she understood the brothers had to have some time alone.

"Hey, Josh, I'm glad you got here safely, but I was just getting ready to run to the store for a few things. I'll be back shortly." She grabbed her purse and coat and headed for the door.

"I suppose you'll take your usual half hour or 45 minutes," Jon remarked.

"Easily, there's always someone who stops me and wants to talk. I got to see Carole the last time. See you two later."

"How do women do that?" Josh asked. "They seem to read us guys like a book. You two are good, you know, and you'll do great with your kids someday, but I'm a little too old to be fooled with the excuse of having to go to the store and you giving her a time limit."

Chuckling, Jon said, "Okay, so you weren't fooled. Come over here and sit down and tell me how things went. From the look on your face, they didn't go too well."

"Oh, they went fine as far as the end result I was going for. Liz, like Christy, read me like a book and did the dirty work for me. She's so awesome, Jon, it is tearing me apart to walk away from her. I told her I wished we could get married right now, but I knew it'd be wrong for her and also wrong in God's eyes."

Seeing the surprise in Jon's eyes, he continued. "Yeah, big brother, I've changed and am trying to get my life on the straight and narrow so I can deserve someone like Liz. After that accident I told you about, I've decided to take a class on the Bible next semester and see what I can learn now that I really want to know what's in that book.

But, back to Liz, all she asked was that we remain friends with an e-mail or phone call now and then and to be able to tolerate each other when we're at the ranch at the same time. Jon, she gave me a kiss after the dance that sent me out of this world. I'd given her a locket and told her I hoped she would wear it and think of me now and then. She realized my meaning when she woke up this morning and then cleared the air so we could eat breakfast at IHOP without anything hanging over our heads. I'd planned to wait until after we were done eating, but I know that neither of us could have eaten a bite if she hadn't, like I said, done the dirty work for me. I'm feeling so empty that all I want to do is drive back up there, take her in my arms and run away with her. How does a person cope with that?"

"All I can say, Josh, is that I know the emptiness. When Christy had her problems and couldn't accept my love as being real, I thought my life was over. I know your situation is different, in a way, but the feelings of loss are the same. I wish I had some magical words I could say that would make it go away, but only God can give you the comfort and peace you need right now. Since you're a changed man, would you like for me to pray with you?"

"I need all the help I can get and I'm really learning that God is always listening when we take time to talk to Him, so here goes: Dear Father in Heaven, the One who has the power and the compassion to make things right, I need your comfort and leading in my life right now. I felt the need to give Liz time and space to enjoy her high school years and for me to grow in my new found faith. Please give me the strength to accept this change and let Liz and me hear your voice and follow closely. Amen."

"Dear Jesus, we are so grateful for this change in Josh's life although it has come with some heartbreak and sadness. In your greatness, may you grant these two precious ones, Liz and Josh, the peace of knowing that you're in charge of their lives, and that things will be all right for those who love and trust You. As Josh has asked, please give him the strength to accept whatever the future holds, and may it bring him happiness and true love. Amen."

They gave each other a brotherly hug and then Josh told him about the weekend. He started with the caught zipper in Liz's dress, which brought a big chuckle as Jon could also relate to those situations at home. He told about the typical high school dance with the boys on one side of the gym and the girls on the other, and then the two attempts of trying to give Liz the locket and the amazing kiss he'd received. He told him about the breakfast and the tour, and going back to the little park where they talked about Christmas, her birthday, and then the memorable goodbye kiss. Finally, he had to tell about the visit from the trooper who turned out to be Liz's cousin.

"Getting to talk to you, Jon, and getting it out in

the open has made me feel a lot more like a human being again. Thanks for listening. Now, what has been happening around here? Anything more on that house you two want to build at the ranch?"

"We've been meeting with an architect in Pueblo and trying to decide just what we want in our home. When it goes up, it'll have to last for a long time, so we need to consider things like the number of bedrooms, baths, how large a kitchen Christy wants, would a family library suffice or do I want a separate room for an office? Noah, of course, has been a great help, as usual. I've never met a man who has so many good ideas and loves to be right in the middle of the whole family affair." He had to chuckle as he remembered back to his honeymoon plans and how going to the secluded family cabin in the mountains had been a fantastic suggestion from Noah, and then he had even made the arrangements with the catering services up there.

"Liz told me that Noah's birthday is the same as mine. Do you suppose that's why I'm so full of ideas?" Josh started laughing and Jon joined in just as he heard the door opening.

"Hey, I'm back. What's all the laughing about?" Christy asked as she came into the room with two sacks of groceries in her arms. Jon jumped up to take one from her and then he followed her into the kitchen.

"Josh was too smart for us. He grasped what we were up to but really appreciated the time to talk to his big brother. What all did you buy, for heaven's sake?"

"Enough to satisfy two big hungry appetites, I hope. Oh, by the way, I saw Carole again and she would like to have us over for a meal before Christmas. She's going to call to see what day would be good for us."

"That's certainly nice of her, but they've hardly had time to get settled. They had such a rough time after losing almost everything in that hurricane. I'm really proud of them for how they're making a new life here and also becoming involved in their church and with their new neighbors. We happened to hear from one of the residents that Erick learned about a family having some wiring problem in one of the older homes. The man had apparently gotten quite a shock plugging an appliance into a faulty outlet. As a good neighbor, Erick went over and offered his help, and from what I understand, he ended up re-wiring a good portion of the house. Noah is going to check into it and make sure Erick didn't incur any of the expenses at the Electric Shop."

A plea from Josh was then clearly heard. "Christy, did you buy any snacks we could munch on before dinner. I didn't stop for lunch, after taking Liz home, so my stomach is now talking to me pretty much like a hungry lion."

"Where have I heard that before?" Christy giggled. "Yes, we have all kinds of snacks to keep your big brother's stomach quiet, Josh, so come on out and see what you can find. I'll start supper shortly, though, so just don't stuff yourself with junk foods."

"Thanks, Sis. Do you mind if I call you that, Christy? It's easier than sister-in-law when I want to call you something besides Christy."

"I don't mind at all having another brother. It makes me feel closer to you, too. I may have to come up with a cute name for you, though."

"Now what did I get myself into? I really need to leave things alone when they're not broken." Laughing, he added, "And you certainly aren't broken."

"Why don't you guys grab some snacks and go into the dining room or living room and I'll get busy fixing dinner as soon as I finish putting these things away."

Christy fixed a wonderful dinner of ham, scalloped potatoes, broccoli, and a great salad of lettuce, celery pieces, mandarin oranges, crisp bacon, and croutons. The dressing was really delicious, but when Josh asked her about it, she'd just smiled and would only say that it was her secret recipe. She'd baked an apple pie earlier for dessert, because she'd known Josh would be coming, but they actually waited until later to enjoy that.

∽

They had talked about playing some Trivia after dinner but then discovered that the Denver Nuggets were being televised. They settled back to watch basketball. By half-time, though, Josh could hardly hold his eyes open so he excused himself and headed next door to bed. He did remind them as he went out the door, "Don't forget to wake me up in the morning so I can go to church with you."

"That is so good to hear," Jon remarked as he quickly pulled Christy into his arms for a wonderful kiss and hug. It wasn't long before he picked her up and carried her to bed without even waiting to find out which team had won.

Josh had forgotten to close the blinds on the double doors that open to the deck from the bedroom, so the sun came in quite early the next morning to wake him up. He was really surprised that he had slept so well, but he attributed it to just being overly tired after hardly any sleep Friday night. In fact, he had been so engrossed with the thought of his upcoming talk with Liz, he wasn't sure he had slept at all.

He joined Jon and Christy for a delicious breakfast, and then they decided to walk to church since it had turned out to be a gorgeous, although quite cold, morning.

Josh was invited to sit with Joseph, Marge, Noah, Eleanor, Brent and Susan during the service, which was the choir's Christmas Cantata. Christy had the solo part in two of the numbers, and she and Jon had also sung a duet. It was a beautiful presentation and Josh was so glad he hadn't missed it.

After a nice lunch at Copland's Restaurant with the Hayes family, Josh reluctantly said his goodbyes and headed home. It was another long melancholy drive since he couldn't stop thinking about the entire weekend--the happy times and the sad times--but they would surely all be memories he would store in his memory bank and never forget. His little princess, he hoped, would now be able to live the next two and a half school years as a carefree teenager loving all the activities that high school offers.

Chapter Fourteen

The week before Christmas had gone by quickly as Josh helped his dad get the hayrack cleaned and covered with fresh straw and bales of hay to sit on, as well as the regular chores. The bells had also gotten polished for the annual trip to cut their tree on Christmas Eve. Now, the grandparents would be arriving soon because they wouldn't think of missing this tradition that had been started the first year Tom and Frances moved to the farm.

The former owners had planted a grove of Frasier Spruce, and with minimum care it has provided Christmas trees every year for them and their close neighbor. Since the weather was usually pretty chilly, they always had blankets to wrap up in, and hot chocolate, coffee, Christmas cookies and homemade fruit cake tucked under the driver's bench.

A few years back, Tom had a chance to buy a used sleigh, so when they have a really nice snow around this time of year, they pull it from the barn and go for sleigh rides during the holidays. They're always hoping for a big snow on Christmas Day, but the latest forecast they heard wasn't calling for any. When was a weatherman ever completely right, though?

Josh had done most of his Christmas shopping that Friday, right after Thanksgiving, when he was doing errands for Jon in the morning and shopping with Liz in the afternoon. Before picking Liz up at the ranch, he'd been in the Jewelry Store with Jon's ring, and he saw a locket he wanted to give Liz for Christmas. He'd not only found that, but had also gotten gifts for his sister, mother, and Christy as well as an idea for Liz's seventeenth birthday. It had been a very successful shopping day because, while with Liz, he'd also found items for the guys in his family. He'd even found gifts for his grandparents, which are usually the hardest. He'd had the stores wrap them so he was all ready for the big day. Of course, finding the locket was the main reason he'd been late getting to the ranch, but he wasn't going to tell Liz that little secret. It had been pure luck that Jon had his survival blanket in the back of his Tahoe so he'd covered those jewelry gifts securely so they wouldn't be seen.

With Christmas on Sunday this year, they would go to the special Christmas service at church and wait until Jon and Christy got there on Monday to open their gifts. He wished Liz would be coming with them, but he had to somehow forget that possibility now that he'd more or less walked away from an involvement in her life.

Liz was in her room wrapping the presents she had purchased. She had to smile as she was wrapping the caps for Grandpa Noah. She remembered how Josh had been the one to suggest them, and had patiently tried on one after another because she couldn't make up her mind. He had finally made the decision for her by saying he was not putting on one more of those caps. He'd then picked up two for her to choose from, and she'd ended up buying both. He'd also suggested the gifts for her dad's birthday which had really been a big hit.

She now picked up the box containing his present, reached up and touched her locket, and felt the tears start to run down her cheeks. She so wished she'd had his gift when he'd given her the locket so she could've seen his face when he'd opened it. She knew that it was impossible now, and she cried softly, "Oh Josh, I miss you so much."

Liz and her family drove down to the ranch on Saturday to deliver the gifts and see all the family. Christmas Eve was always a great time when they all climbed aboard the hayrack and went to cut the tree. The only thing missing this year was the snow, but the forecast for tomorrow had promised a white blanket. "I hope the snow at Thanksgiving isn't our only one this year," Joseph remarked as they were rambling along toward the tree farm.

When they got back and the tree was being decorated by too many hands, Christy took Liz to the library and asked, "Liz, how are you doing? Josh was a basket case when he got to our place last Saturday, but he felt better after he'd had a heart to heart talk with Jon. Have you had someone to talk to or could I be your shoulder?"

"Thanks, Christy. The whole family knows the situation and has been wonderful, as far as they can be. I can't understand my feelings completely because Josh was so frustrating at times. I do miss him, though, because it seems so final. I understand why he felt he had to do this, but it doesn't make me feel any better. I just wish I could be there when he opens my gift, but I know I can't so I'll try to concentrate on the rest of the family."

"I went through the same feelings when I couldn't

accept Jon's love as being true and unyielding, but I didn't have your problem of waiting over two years to graduate from high school. It must be terribly frustrating, but a lot can happen in two years."

"That's just one of the things I'm concerned about. Josh is too good a person not to be snatched up by a girl who is old enough and also ready to get married. Did you know that he wished we could get married right now, but he said it wouldn't be right for me or with God, so he forced himself to walk away? I have to accept the fact that my first love is gone."

"I'm so sorry, Liz. I wish you didn't have to go through this when you are still so young. If there is anything I can do to help, please let me know."

"There is one thing, Christy. When he opens my gift, will you watch his face and tell me what his expression was like? I love to watch while people open their gifts, because you can easily tell if they like it or not. Would you do that for me, please?"

"I'll be happy to do that, Liz. If I could steal you away from your family, I'd take you along with us, but I'm afraid that's out of the question this year." They then returned to see the six guys standing back and admiring their handiwork. The tree did look beautiful, and they'd also put garlands around the doorway between the living room and dining room and the lights were blinking like twinkling stars.

Marge then summoned them to come around the piano, and as she played several of their favorite Christmas carols, they'd all joined in singing. Joseph, of course, had gotten the Bible and began his annual reading of the Christmas story from the book of Luke. He ended with just a short prayer for peace in the world and a safe trip for all those traveling.

David and Rachel announced that they'd better be heading for home so they would be able to enjoy Christmas Day without falling asleep. Brad, at 20 years old, had to add that he was going to wait for Santa to land on the rooftop this year and finally see those eight flying reindeer. He'd then burst out laughing when they all stared at him. Shaking their heads, his family grabbed their coats, gave everyone a Christmas hug, and then they were on their way.

Brent left shortly after that to take Susan home and Noah, Joseph, and Jon sat down to visit while Eleanor, Marge and Christy went to fix hot chocolate and cookies. It was going on 10 o'clock when Noah announced that it was past his bed time, took Eleanor's hand in his and prepared to leave.

Marge spoke up, "Since we don't have any little ones, yet, to get up early for, I was thinking that we might go to the church service in the morning and then open our gifts after lunch. Would you all agree with that?"

Jon put a pout on his lips and answered, "You mean I don't get to open my gift from Santa the first thing in the morning?" They all had a good laugh but shortly headed to their separate rooms.

∽

A similar scene was taking place at the Holcomb farm. The tree had finally gotten decorated by Josh, Jacob, and Janice while their grandparents, along with their mom and dad, were all giving instructions. Even without Jon there helping, it had turned out pretty well and the lights were actually all burning, which was a bit unusual for them. Someone had found a twig of mistletoe and had hung it from the chandelier, so the fun of family hugs and a few kisses had to begin. Matthew had just dropped by so, of course, he got to enjoy that part of the evening with a kiss or two from Janice.

Frances finally put a halt to that by going to the piano and beginning to play the old favorite carols, and they had soon gathered around the piano to sing. The grandparents' voices weren't what they used to be, but a fun time was had by all. Eggnog, with more fruit cake and cookies soothed their tired singing throats, and after Tom had read a new Christmas story from a magazine, they called it a night.

When Josh got to his room, he started remembering the night Liz had opened her gift and the unbelievable kiss he'd received from her. He got ready for bed and was hugging his pillow tight when, in his prayer, he asked that they both would be able to enjoy the blessings of the season and Jesus coming as a babe to save them from sin. His pillow was wet with tears as he tried to understand how the right thing to do could make him so miserable.

༅

Liz lay awake with her thoughts of Josh. Was he sleeping soundly without even a thought of her anymore or was he having a hard time sleeping, too? She suddenly sat up in bed and pondered if she could reach him on his cell phone or was it already too late to call? She just knew she wouldn't sleep until she'd heard his voice.

She reached for the phone, hesitated a few seconds, but then dialed his number before she could change her mind. It rang one, two, three, four times and then, "Merry Christmas, I guess, whoever you are." His voice sounded so different and somewhat sad as if he'd possibly been crying. She almost hung up, but she'd gone this far, she had to go all the way. "Josh, it's Liz. I couldn't get to sleep, after we got back from the ranch, and I decided I needed to hear my friend's voice. I hope I didn't do the wrong thing again. I seem to be making a lot of weird mistakes lately. Did you have a nice Christmas Eve with your family?"

"Hey Liz, I've been holding you in my arms for a good hour, even though it was just my pillow. I've been trying to understand why I feel so sad, when in my heart I know I've done the right thing. To answer your question, though, we did go and cut the tree and got it decorated. It was different without Jon, but we survived. How was your trip to the ranch?"

"It was fun, I guess. It was hard for me, in a way, because every time I looked at Jon, I thought of you and wanted to cry. Christy talked to me, while the guys were decorating the tree, but words don't make the emptiness go away. I guess time will help, and maybe getting back in school will, too, but it's hard to grasp that you're out of my life"

"I hope I'm not out of your life completely, Liz. We'll be seeing each other at the ranch from time to time, and I do hope we can remain good friends."

"I guess that *is* something to look forward to, but I'd better let you get some sleep now. Please keep in touch with me, Josh. We did promise each other that much."

"I'm glad you called, Sweetheart, and I will keep in touch, but it's not going to make it any easier, you know."

"Oh, I'm sorry, Josh. I didn't realize you'd rather we make a clean break. If that's what you want, please tell me in an e-mail. I'll just say Merry Christmas and

Goodnight for now." There was a click and she was gone.

Maybe that would be the best solution, Liz, but I can't do that, not right now anyway. I'm afraid you've become a little too precious for me to leave our friendship in the unsavory predicament you just put it in.

Chapter Fifteen

The next morning, Josh was still upset about the abrupt ending of the call from Liz, and he hadn't slept well at all. However, he forced himself to listen to the pastor as he told the story of Mary and Joseph and the birth of Jesus. He realized a lot of work had been done to set the stage. A nice door frame and fancy door represented the Inn, and a framed manger with straw, a cradle, and a big star shining above was a good facsimile of where the Christ child had been born.

Members of the Diaconate portrayed Joseph and Mary, the innkeeper and his wife, the shepherds and the wise men as the pastor narrated a beautifully written story using the familiar Bible verses and some poems. It was very impressive and Josh learned quite a bit more than his 'know-it-all' attitude had always thought he knew.

After returning home, his mom and grandmothers fixed a light lunch and then Josh and Jacob offered to clean up the dishes. When they were finished with that, they saddled their horses and took the annual Christmas ride together although it seemed a little strange without Jon. They were both looking forward to the newlywed's arrival tomorrow.

The grasses were crackling under the horses' hoofs from last night's frost, and the sky actually looked like they could get some sleet or even snow. They'd been riding for about 45 minutes when they realized they were near the piglets' enclosure. They decided to stop and check the temperature and the feed which might possibly save their dad a trip, but they found it was down to 50 degrees. Since it should be around 65 to 70, they quickly checked several areas hoping to find the problem, because they knew the shelter would cool down quickly in this weather. They finally discovered that one of the fans was stuck and it had apparently cut off all the power, which, of course, had also shut down the heating unit. They tried to correct it by disconnecting the one fan but still had no luck getting the heating unit to restart without any tools, so they headed home on a gallop to notify their dad. Josh, of course, realized there was another phase of farming that he'd have to learn more about--electricity.

Matthew was just returning from his parents, where he had spent Christmas Day, so had dropped by to see Janice on the way to his apartment. He'd just overheard a part of the conversation between the two guys and their dad, but he soon realized there was an electrical problem someplace. When he noticed the concern in Mr. Holcomb's eyes and saw that he was getting his coat on, he quickly walked over to him and said, "I'll go with you, Tom, and we'll see if my studies in electricity will prove helpful."

"I'd appreciate that, Matthew, although I'd forgotten that you'd taken a course in the electrical field. I guess Janice will forgive you if you can help save a bunch of piglets from possible death." Grinning, the two walked out the door together.

Josh and Jacob were getting warmed up with hot chocolate when they realized they hadn't stalled the horses because of the hurry to let their dad know about the heat in the shelter. They'd heard the truck go by the window, and they knew that the tool box which contains every farm tool imaginable was now on its way to the rescue. "Do you want to ride out there again to see how it's going?" Josh asked.

"I'd just be in the way, and I'd really appreciate it if you would stall Lightning for me. I feel like I got chilled out there riding and I think I should take an aspirin and just lie down for awhile. I don't want to be sick tomorrow when Christy and Jon get here."

"Sure thing, Jacob. Make sure you put enough covers over you and get some rest. I may do the same thing since I didn't sleep very well last night."

"I heard your cell phone ring after you went to your room last night. Was it a little love message from Liz or a final goodbye?"

"That's only for me to know, Little Brother. Now, scoot and get to bed. I'll tend to the horses and then see if I can get a little shut eye, too."

෴

Liz had finally fallen asleep about 4 a.m. after pacing the floor and trying to under-stand why God was putting her and Josh through this ordeal. She had hung up on him last night because she couldn't stand to hear the sadness in his voice. That had probably been a mistake, but it was better than just sobbing over the phone. She wanted to help him through this separation, not make it worse. She glanced at the clock on her nightstand and realized it was almost 9 o'clock and no one had awakened her. She showered quickly and dressed for the church service, but she had little hope of hearing a single word.

She found the family at the breakfast table but dressed in sweat pants and sweaters. It wasn't normal for them not to be dressed for church. "What's going on?" she asked as she sat down at her place beside her dad.

"The Christmas service at the church has been cancelled because the furnace went out and there's no heat. As long as we wouldn't be going anyplace, we didn't wake you. It was pretty late last night when we heard you still up, so we thought you probably needed the rest. Did you happen to call Josh last night?" her father asked as he was studying her puffy eyes.

"Yes, but it didn't last long. I couldn't stand the sadness in his voice, and he said my calling wouldn't make it any easier, so I hung up. I know now that it was probably wrong, but I didn't want to start crying and sobbing over the phone. I'll explain the next time we talk, if there is a next time." She was up and out of the room so quickly, the family wasn't sure how to react.

"I don't think I've ever seen a first love so traumatic, which makes me wonder if it's really more than a first love," Rachel remarked. "Does God really feel they need this time apart to fully understand the deep love they have for one another? Christy told me that Josh had mentioned to Jon that he was taking a course on the Bible this second semester because he wants to feel he deserves someone like Liz.

Their relationship certainly hasn't been an easy one so far. He actually made her so angry at times, she thought she hated him," she laughed, "but they just continued to end up together. She loved being in Hayes and having fun doing things with him, and they kept growing closer all the time. I just pray there aren't harder roads ahead that God is preparing them for. My heart aches to see them both so miserable and nothing they can do about it, but I do have to admire Josh for what he did. Maybe when school starts up again, there will be other things to get involved in and that will lessen the loss."

"They are two very strong individuals, Rachel, and we'll just have to do a lot more praying on their behalf. I've been very impressed with the young man, and I know he has a good Christian background, the same as Jon. He admits he was a rebel, of sorts, but if he wants to change so he can deserve someone like Liz, he is something special in my book. Whether he and Liz finally get together or not, I wish him all the luck in the world."

Brad and Mary had been listening to their parent's conversation, but had remained quiet. Brad finally spoke up, "I really like Josh, but I think Liz is just too young to be doing any thinking about a relationship. She has over two years of school left before she even graduates from high school, so why don't you put your foot down? Make her cut all ties with Josh, and stick to the rules you've set about dating."

"You are so immature, Brad. No wonder you've never had a girlfriend, and you're a senior in college," Mary retorted. "Why don't you look around and find a nice girl for your-self? You might understand then that when love is meant to be, it's meant to be. I'm sorry Liz is going through a hard separation, but she at least has had a lot of fun with Josh and has certainly grown up a lot more than you have."

"All right, that's enough. This isn't the time to be throwing insults or orders around. Knowing our Liz, she'll handle this whole situation with her usual poise and grace. Let's leave it at that and try to have a family togetherness that we can all enjoy. Do you suppose one of you could bring the coffee to the table so Mother and I could have another cup?"

"Sure, Dad." Mary was on her way to the coffeemaker just as Liz was returning to the kitchen. She had changed clothes and was also in her sweat pants and a matching top. She glanced out the window and realized that it had snowed last night after they'd gotten home, so all of a sudden, she wanted to have a snowball fight and to also make an angel in the snow. She persuaded Mary and Brad to go outside with her, and it was definitely the distraction she needed. She'd given her siblings quite a pounding by the time they'd called it quits, and she was more relaxed and smiling when they came in all covered with snow.

❧

Josh and Jacob both felt refreshed when they got up and dressed for the Christmas feast that had been prepared while they'd slept away a big part of the afternoon. They also learned that their dad and Matt had been able to fix the fan and get the heater going again so everything looked good with the piglets.

Since Matt had moved into the apartment above the barn and was working full time, he was asked to join them for meals quite often, but he certainly hadn't planned to stay for the Christmas dinner. He didn't think he needed anymore after the meal he had eaten at his folks' at noon. The grandparents had insisted, however, that he sit down and eat a little something with them. "After all, you're a growing boy," Grandma Shelley had remarked. To them, he had become one of their grandsons, and they adored him.

Monday came and with it the expectation of Jon and Christy's arrival. When it was only 11 o'clock when they pulled in, everyone was shocked but extremely happy. Jon told them they'd started about 6:30 this morning, and since the roads were deserted, they'd made real good time.

When there was a break in the hugs and welcomes, Jon then took Christy to show her their room and freshen up a little. When they returned to the living room, everyone but the grandmothers and Frances was seated around the tree.

They thought they could open their presents now, but it wasn't going to happen quite yet. Frances had come to the door and announced that they had prepared a lunch of all the Christmas dinner leftovers. "Jon and Christy are most likely hungry since they were up so early this morning, so let's eat first."

Josh teasingly blamed Jon for this delay, but he was rather hungry himself. They caught up on news from both families while they ate and then eagerly tackled the pile of presents under the tree which seemed to take forever.

When Josh was handed the gift from Liz, Christy's eyes were glued to his face so she could tell Liz how he had reacted. Josh, however, glanced to see who it was from and then put it down beside him. "I can't open this one right now," was all he said, but when all the presents had been opened, he picked it up and left the room.

Opening Liz's gift was one of the hardest things he had ever done. He just wanted to be beside her so he could respond with a kiss like the one he'd received after she'd seen the locket. He very slowly unwrapped the package, opened the nice felt covered box, and inside found an ID bracelet with his name on the front and "The Mysterious Princess" on the back. She'd included a note which read, "As you said to me, Josh, I hope you'll wear it and think of me now and then. Always, Liz." It was a beautiful piece of jewelry, and he knew he would wear it every day but only if he could think of her every day without his heart completely breaking in two.

Jon appeared at the door and asked if he could come in. Josh nodded and waved his big brother into the room. He held up the bracelet for him to see and also the note.

"She asked Christy to watch your face when you opened her gift because she loves to see the expression on people's faces. She says she can tell if they really like the gift or not by the look on their face. What should Christy tell her?"

"Have Christy tell her I wouldn't open it in front of the family. It had to be done in private, since she wasn't here to share the moment like I was when she received the locket. I plan to call her later and explain, so Christy doesn't have to worry." He then went on to tell Jon about the phone call last night and the abrupt ending. "I can't understand why she did that, or what she was thinking, but I plan to find out. We can't let it end on that note."

"Do you feel it's really over, Josh, or is God just giving the two of you some time to figure out your true feelings and maybe for Liz to get a little older?"

"Two and a half years is a long time, Jon, and I have no idea what might happen in that time. I've decided to look around a little when I get to school, and I hope Liz does, too. It might break the closeness we feel right now, or it will draw us even closer. We'll just have to wait and see. I just know that the feelings I have for her are nothing like I've felt with any other girls I've dated."

It was dusk when they got back to the living room, and they found almost everyone looking out the big picture window. "What's going on?" Jon asked.

"It's snowing," Janice whispered with a big smile on her face. "Dad and Matt have gone out to get the sleigh from the barn. The way that snow is falling, it shouldn't be too long before there's enough on the ground so we can take a sleigh ride. I hope you and your wife brought some heavy clothes. If not, I'm sure we can find something for you to put on so you can join us," she giggled.

"I believe we came prepared, Little Sister, but it'll certainly be an added thrill to get to enjoy a sleigh ride this year."

∽

"Our family can't grow too much more, or we'll have to make two trips," Tom was chuckling as everyone climbed aboard. All twelve spaces were filled now but the closeness helped create more warmth as

171

the snow was still falling. "It's such an exciting treat, though, because it doesn't happen too often."

"When you need more space, Tom, I think we grandparents will gladly give up our seats to the younger set," Grandfather Holcomb replied, "but we'll enjoy it one last time."

"You're not going to give up your seat, Gramps. These little gals will fit very nicely on our laps when that time comes," Jon retorted as he gave Christy a big hug and pulled her closer. "Can't have you getting cold now, can we?" he chuckled as he gave her a little peck on the nose and wrapped the blanket more snugly around her. Of course, that little romantic gesture did not escape Josh's watchful eye, and he felt a tear run down his cheek as he only wished Liz were here in his arms.

It was a wonderful evening for a sleigh ride as the snow fell in big flakes that were just gorgeous to watch. Christmas cookies and hot apple cider were enjoyed as they moved along, and the jingle of the bells that had been transferred from the hayrack to the sleigh, put everyone in the mood to sing. They were doing a great harmonizing job on Silent Night when they arrived in the tiny town near the farm. Many of the residents came out to wave and wish them a Merry Christmas when they heard the singing and the jingling of the bells even though it wasn't Christmas Eve or even Christmas Day. It was, however, a special

Christmas Day for this family, and what a wonderful and marvelous way to end it. They were all so thankful for getting the opportunity to go sleigh riding, but it was extra special for being together as a family.

When they returned, a fire was started in the fireplace and bowls were filled with homemade soup to warm them up. A few marshmallows were roasted while they sat in the warmth of the fire and the conversation continued to catch everyone up on more recent happenings that had been missed previously such as the house plans for Jon and Christy.

It wasn't long until the grandparents excused themselves. "Well, I guess we won't have to get up at daybreak in the morning since the presents have all been opened. I'll bet Santa was a little confused when he landed at this house this year," Grandpa Holcomb chuckled as he held his wife's hand and headed for the bedroom they had been using every Christmas for the last twenty-six years. Grandpa Shelley just smiled and said, "Goodnight All. It's been a wonderful Christmas. We'll see you again in the morning before we head for home."

After another hour or so, everyone was heading to bed but was looking forward to another day with more togetherness. Christy, however, had a phone call to make before she called it a night although she wasn't sure what she was going to say.

Chapter Sixteen

The phone could be heard ringing when Liz and her family pulled into the garage. They were returning from a musical program that had been held at the Civic Center to raise money to fund the Red Cross. Their many charitable activities, especially all the disasters that have befallen our own country these past few months, had made it Rachel's favorite charity and she had helped get several celebrities to agree to perform. It had been a great success and, of course, she was very pleased.

Liz jumped from the car as soon as it had stopped. She hurried into the house to see if she could catch whoever was calling. Just as she reached it, however, the connection was broken. She checked the Caller ID and saw that it was from the Holcomb farm, so it had to be Christy or Josh, and Josh would probably use his cell phone. She didn't know whether to call back or wait for whoever had called to try again, but it didn't require a decision when the phone began ringing again. She quickly picked it up to answer, "Becker residence."

"Hey, Liz, did you just get home, or did I really dial the wrong number before? The ring just didn't sound right, so I thought I'd misdialed."

Liz recognized Christy's voice. "We were just pulling into the garage when I heard the phone, but I couldn't reach it before you cut off."

"It's probably the difference in the reception down here. I really wanted to talk to you, so I'm glad I decided to try again."

"We attended the fundraiser for the Red Cross tonight, which was fabulous, by the way. You wouldn't believe the singers that Mom helped convince to perform. So, how is everything down there? Did you get any snow at the ranch before you left? We got a nice snow here Saturday night so I talked Mary and Brad into having a snowball fight yesterday morning since the heat had gone out at our church and the service had to be cancelled. A good snowball fight was just what I needed to get my mind off Josh for awhile."

"No, the snow missed us at the ranch unless they got some today after we left. We did get a rare snow here, though, and we got to go for a sleigh ride tonight which was lots of fun. Everyone has gone to bed now except me. I haven't seen much of the farm yet, but the house is lovely. I know that isn't what you want to hear, but I was impressed. As to your request, though, I couldn't complete your wish because Josh left the room with your gift unopened. Jon went to see if he was okay, and he told Jon that he would be calling you to clear up a few things, but that I should tell you that he couldn't open your gift in front of the family. He really wanted you beside him so he could respond with a kiss like you gave him when you had seen the locket. That kiss of yours must have made quite an impression on him. Jon says he has mentioned it several times."

"Yeah, well, it doesn't matter how impressive it was anymore. We're going our own separate ways now and what happens, happens. He told me Christmas Eve that keeping in touch wasn't going to make it any easier, so I told him to e-mail me with his wishes and I hung up on him. I realize that was wrong, but I couldn't stand his sad voice and I was so afraid I was going to cry. I still believe my life is in God's hands, Christy, and even though I don't understand it right now, I'm sure it will turn out for the best just because it will be God's plan. Did you get to see the bracelet or did he hide it somewhere, too?"

"Oh, yes, I got to see it and it's beautiful. He's

wearing it and I notice him touching it quite often. He drops his hand like he is trying to understand just why something is on his arm, or maybe why you aren't beside him. I have a feeling Josh is one confused young man right now. He hasn't mentioned that you hung up on him, though, unless he's told Jon. We haven't had the opportunity to discuss his visit with Josh because of the sleigh ride and all the family around. I'm praying that God helps both of you find a happy solution to this problem you're facing."

"Don't hold your breath, Christy. I'm going back to school and try my best to get on the Spanish team that is going to Spain over spring break. Maybe I'll meet someone on the team, or even in Spain, that will give me the answers I need. Josh has to become my past, I guess, and the sooner I accept that, the sooner it should make it easier to move on. He even remarked once that I might find a handsome Spaniard while I'm over there."

"Maybe that *is* the answer, Liz, but I just can't forget how close you two were and how you complemented each other in so many ways. I'd better let you go, though, because it's getting late and I'm told it's early to rise around here. Goodnight, Liz, and you know you'll definitely be in my prayers."

"Thanks, Christy, and have a great time down there. Please tell all of them that I send my best wishes for the remainder of the holidays. Goodnight."

❧

It was almost noon the next day when the grandparents left for their homes. It was after a long leisurely breakfast with lots of coffee and a conversation that certainly didn't want to stop. The days then passed rather quickly as Jon showed Christy the highlights of his growing-up years. She had met some of his long-time friends, saw the schools he'd attended, entered their quaint little church, and scouted the layout of the farm. He'd taken her riding over the snow-covered fields and told her stories about his youth, which were both humorous and traumatic.

It was wonderful getting more acquainted with Jon's parents and siblings, and when Friday arrived, she certainly wasn't ready to start thinking about leaving. They'd decided to start back early Saturday morning so they could avoid those wild drivers who are always out on New Year's Eve, especially when it falls on the weekend.

❧

After Christy had called Monday night, Liz waited for the call Christy had said Josh was going to make, but the phone didn't ring. She'd also checked her e-mail several times each day but there was no message. By Friday, she'd decided he wasn't going to call, so she went shopping with Mary and her mother. She'd exchanged a sweater and skirt outfit, that didn't fit well, for a nice wool jacket that would go with almost everything. She was in a much better mood when they got back home because she'd always enjoyed shopping.

She went to her room to hang up the new jacket and then noticed her Bible lying by the bed. She realized she hadn't even opened it for several days, and that really wasn't like her. She sat down and read for a few minutes and then made a New Year's resolution that she would not forget to read her Bible every day.

She'd changed into her comfy sweats for the evening and had picked up her Bible to read again when she heard the phone ring. "Someone else can answer it this time since it won't be for me," she mumbled to herself, but then she heard Mary calling and saying she had a phone call. Thinking it was probably one of her school friends, she answered quite cheerfully, "Hey, what's up?"

"You sound pretty chipper tonight, Liz. Have you found a new love already? I'm sorry I've disappointed you if you were expecting someone else."

"Oh, Hi, Josh. Mary didn't say who was calling, but I really wasn't expecting it to be you. I thought you'd probably have better things to do with your time by now."

"Hold it right there, Miss Becker. I've been trying

to get my head on straight, but you know Jon and Christy have been here, and it hasn't been easy. They're leaving early in the morning, but I want to get some things settled with you before we both go back to our respective schools. First, I want to thank you for the ID bracelet. It was a perfect gift. I'll wear it and probably think of you more than just now and then. I did, however, miss the kiss I wish I could've enjoyed after opening it.

Second, I want to know why you hung up on me Christmas Eve. I'd been hugging my pillow, pretending it was you, and also praying that God will lead us into some happier times during the next two years. I heard your voice, got one or two sentences out of my mouth, and then you were gone. What gives, Liz?"

"I guess it was another of my many mistakes. I thought you sounded so sad and I didn't want to start crying on the phone and make you feel worse, so I hung up. I'm sorry, Josh, but I don't know if I can handle talking to you anymore, or seeing you, because it just hurts too much. I have to get on with my life without you, and I guess the best way to do that is to make a clean break. What do you think?"

"I think it's impossible. We're connected by family now, and we'll be forced to see each other now and then. You remember, don't you, that you were the one who wanted to remain friends and try to tolerate each other at the ranch. Have you changed your mind about that? I know it'll be a little hard, but we won't see each other that often, so I'll sure try if you will. I really would like to have you as my friend."

"Here we go again. I can just see your big brown eyes probably twinkling and also waiting for the answer that you're expecting to hear. But, Josh, how can I agree to be just a friend when I've realized that I want so much more than that with you?"

"You've never admitted that to me before, Princess, even when I told you I wished we could get married right away and I would love you for the rest of my life. After that big confession on my part, which I guess I should never have uttered, I thought you acted as if it meant nothing to you. Now, it appears, we have just added another unsolvable problem to our dilemma.

Princess, you know I want you to enjoy your high school years and have a chance to look around and see who and what is out there. I know you're really looking forward to the trip to Spain and France, as well as other facets of learning at the high school level, and as much as I adore you, I couldn't take that away from you. So, why don't we remain friends with no heavy commitments, find out what is out there waiting for us, and let God be our Guide? Do you think you would be willing to try until we see each other again at least?"

"I'm a little confused right now, but I know what you've said is probably right, so I'll try to stay friends with you as we go looking for a silver lining, as that old song says. I did realize, though, after the feelings I had that one night with you, Josh, that I learned a lot about what I want and who I want. My life is in God's hands, however, and it helps to know that He still knows the end of our story. He knows exactly what's going to happen and has known since we were born."

"Those feelings were the first of their kind for you, Princess, and there will most likely be many more. I'm really glad I could give you an insight of what love can mean to a person, and I wish I could be the one to share all those intimate feelings, but only God knows what we'll experience in the coming years. I just ask that you don't give yourself to anyone until you have a wedding ring and marriage certificate in your possession."

"I do feel better since this talk with you, Josh, and I think I can actually go to sleep tonight. When are you returning to school?"

"I plan to drive over on Tuesday, the 3rd, so I can sign up for the Bible class, and then my classes start on the 5th. What about you?"

"Our classes start on the 3rd, and I can just imagine the homework they'll pile on that first week. Do you think you'll still need help with your Spanish?"

"Let's see how things go, Liz. I may have already gotten enough help from you so I can master it by myself. I did do pretty well on the exam before vacation. Now, we'll see if I can remember what I learned," he chuckled. "Maybe I'll call and talk to you, now and then, in Spanish."

"That would be fun to try anyway. Well, I'll wish you good luck, Josh, and let's be sure to keep God in our lives."

"Definitely. And listen, Princess, you have a great 17th birthday and a very good second half of the school year. I'll probably be talking to you or sending you an e-mail before your birthday, and I'll still be holding you in my dreams. Remember you'll always be My Sweet, Wonderful, and Mysterious Princess."

"Thanks, Josh. You'll probably be in my dreams, too. Please remember--don't do too much celebrating on New Year's Eve, especially if you're out driving."

"I'll probably be in bed before the clock strikes twelve. Goodnight, Liz, and may we both have a very Happy New Year."

As Liz was starting to open her Bible to read, she prayed instead. "Lord Jesus, you who knows all things, please bring a little hope to my troubled mind. I'm feeling so alone tonight, but I do believe you have my life in your hands, so I ask for just a little assurance to sustain me through this time of my life." She let the

Bible open on its own and was surprised to have it open to the 3rd chapter of Proverbs. The same verses that had come to her in the car after Thanksgiving were the first she saw as she glanced at the open page, but she read them again very slowly so she could really concentrate on the true meaning.

'Trust in the Lord with all your heart and lean not on your own understanding; in all your ways acknowledge Him and He will make your paths straight.' *Thank you, Jesus, you must really want me to remember those words as you have given them to me three times in my life now. I'll definitely rely on that promise because I trust You and your word for the guidance of my future.*

∽

There were some teary goodbyes Saturday morning as Jon and Christy prepared to leave, especially when it came time to say goodbye to Josh. Jon had whispered something in his ear, but Josh had only nodded and then had quickly slipped away.

"I can't leave like this, Christy. I'm going to find him and try to do something to bring the old Josh back. Say a little prayer, will you please?"

"Of course, Jon. Take all the time you need."

Jon found Josh in his room, lying on the bed and staring up at the ceiling. "Josh, can we talk before I have to leave?"

"I thought we'd already said goodbye. I'll be all right, Jon. The sooner I accept the fact that you're married, Liz is probably not in my life anymore, and my future right now is at school, everything will get back in sync. It's not like we haven't been apart before. You were at law school for those three years, for heaven's sake, and I've been away in college, too. I survived those years, and I'll survive now."

"I just couldn't leave without knowing that you're going to be all right. Things are a little different right now, and you and I both know it. We've always been able to talk about anything, Josh, and I'm here now if you need to get something off your chest."

"I know, Jon, but everything will be fine. I talked to Liz last night. We're on the same track, and we're going to try to remain friends. How that will go for sure, nobody knows, but that's our problem, and we're old enough to work it out. You go on home now before all those wild celebrations start tonight."

They shared a promise to stay in touch, a brotherly hug, a slap on the back, and then Jon was gone, but not without a prayer for his brother who he knew was struggling with a new found faith, a lost love, and a separation from his family while at college. It's a lot for anyone to cope with at the same time.

After Jon had gone, Josh picked up his Bible and let it fall open. He read from the 31st chapter of

Deuteronomy: "Do not be afraid or terrified because of them, for the Lord your God goes with you; he will never leave you nor forsake you; do not be discouraged."

He couldn't keep from smiling because he knew for sure now that God had accepted him back in his arms, and like Liz, his life was in God's hands.

Chapter Seventeen

Liz was a little more excited than she'd expected when she got to school Tuesday morning. Spanish was her 2nd period and she was looking forward to learning if she'd be included in the team going to Spain. When she reached the classroom door, she was so nervous that her hands were shaking. She wanted to be chosen so badly, because she felt the extra work that would be required, and also preparing for the trip, would help keep her mind off Josh. She had to think of other things to do before she went completely crazy.

She noticed a note on the blackboard: "The following students are to immediately report to Room 200 for further instructions." She very quickly scanned the list, and when she saw her name she couldn't resist pumping her fist and yelling "Yes!" She headed for Room 200. Several others were there when she arrived, but only one from her class.

She noticed a boy standing over by the window, and he'd watched her closely as she came into the room. She couldn't recall ever seeing him around school before so she was wondering what he was doing here. He was really quite handsome with his wavy dark hair, brown eyes, probably about 5'10" tall, and also very nicely dressed.

She joined her classmate but occasionally glanced over at him. He hadn't taken his eyes off her, which made her a little nervous. She decided to find out who he was and just what he was up to. Her friend refused to go with her, so she approached this stranger by herself. "I'm Elizabeth Becker, better known as Liz," she started the conversation. "I don't think I've seen you around school before today. Are you new here, or are you going to be helping with the trip or teaching this class?"

"I wish I were smart enough to be the teacher," he smiled, "but my family moved here over the holidays so it's my first day at this school. We came from Akron, Ohio."

"Oh, then I extend a welcome to a new city and a new school. It must be hard to change from one school to another when you're so close to graduation. Did you have to leave a lot of friends you'd made growing up?"

"My family has moved several times during my school years so I learned not to get too close to anyone, because I knew I'd probably be moving again. Since I'm a junior now, I'm hoping I'll get to stay through graduation this time. Oh, my name is Sergio Silvano. My grandparents are originally from Spain, and they've been trying to teach me Spanish for quite a few years now. They want me to visit their homeland someday and be able to speak the language, so I finally decided, back in 9th grade, that it would be to my advantage to take a class with a real good teacher. It helped a lot, so when I enrolled here and heard about this trip to Spain, I talked to the teacher about the requirements. Hopefully, if I'm lucky, I can be included. Have you studied Spanish long?"

"This is only my second year of Spanish, but I've also been studying French. They're both very interesting and I'm enjoying the challenge. Oh, here comes the teacher now." She started off to find a desk, sensed him following her, so graciously found two together.

"Thanks, Liz, for being so nice and welcoming me to your school. I assure you, it doesn't happen very often."

Liz listened carefully as the teacher explained that only sixteen would be selected to make the trip after they'd completed the assignment she was giving them today. She'd told them before, but reiterated that they would be speaking Spanish most of the time they were gone. She'd also have forms for them to be filled out and signed by their parents, and then returned as soon as possible with the amount stated. There would most likely be three adult chaperones, they'd leave on Saturday, the first day of spring break, and return the following weekend. There were a few questions, of course, and then the period was over. Liz was so excited as she headed for the door to go to her next class, but then she heard Sergio call her name. "Do you have anyone that you study with?" he asked. "I was thinking that maybe we could help each other by studying together, if you don't already have a study mate. We found that quite helpful in Akron, and we also practiced speaking the language while we studied."

"Oh . .well. . .it probably would help, but what exactly did you have in mind? I guess we could meet in the library during our free hour or right after school for awhile."

"That would be a good start, but the library is so quiet it would be a little difficult to practice any conversation. Maybe I could come to your house once or twice a week, if your parents don't object. I could have my dad call and vouch for me. He just became the new President of the West Side Bank. What's your father's occupation?"

"My father is a Pediatrician and has his office at the hospital. I'm sure there'd be no problem if I decide this is what I'd like to do. Let's try the library this afternoon and see how things go. I have to get to my next class now, so I'll see you later."

As she scurried down the hallway, all kinds of thoughts were going through her mind. *Oh, Liz, what have you done now? This guy shows up out of the blue, wants to start studying together, and you fall for it. He had a good excuse about just moving here, which I could easily check, and surely the teacher knows something about him. He was on the list to go on the trip anyway, and I can't help but wonder if this could be another quick answer to one of my prayers. I **was** asking for something to do to help me forget about Josh. Sergio certainly isn't bad looking although he might be a little too much like Josh with the dark hair and dark brown eyes, but not quite as tall. Well, I'll just be very careful until he can prove himself to be trustworthy.*

❧

After her last class, Liz hurried toward the library. She was anxious to see if Sergio would really show up and how this studying together would go. She'd been thinking, for a while now, that she'd love to have someone to talk to in Spanish. Josh had mentioned that he might call and talk to her in Spanish, but she doesn't feel that is going to happen now. Sergio, however, said he'd been studying since 9th grade and he's a junior now. He's had at least a year more of study than she has, plus all the help he said he'd received from his grandparents.

He'll be so far ahead of me that I'll be lost trying to keep up with him. Why did I agree to this, anyway? Maybe I should forget it and go on home. Just then she turned the corner into the hallway where the library is located. She glanced down the hall and, of course, there he was coming around the corner from another hallway and heading her way. He had a big smile on his face.

I'll never live this down if I make a fool of myself, but just then they met just outside the library door.

"Hi, Liz, that was good timing. Are you ready to hit the books, or would you like to get something to drink first?"

"It depends on how long you want to study. The librarian only stays until 4 or 4:30 and it's 2:45 now, so maybe we'd better study for awhile and then get something to drink. Is that OK?"

"That's great. Let's go in and get started." He led the way into the library and found a table away from the others in a rather secluded area. "This looks pretty darn good, don't you think?"

"It should give us a little more privacy and maybe

we *will* be able to talk to each other in Spanish as we study. Getting settled at the table, Liz then asked, "Where do you think we should start? Do you want to look at the assignment the teacher gave us this morning first or should we do some reviewing? I'm a little afraid that you're going to be way ahead of me."

"Possibly not. I've found that each teacher has a different method of teaching." They discussed where each had been in the study book at Christmas break, checked quite a few of the last words they had studied, and Liz realized she wasn't as far behind as she'd assumed she would be. *His previous teachers must have moved more slowly through the book*, she was thinking when he suggested they take a look at the assignment. They were deep in this discussion when the librarian came to inform them it was 4:30 and she had to close. They were amazed that the time had gone by so fast, but they agreed that they had made a good dent in their work.

Sergio walked with her to her locker to get the books she needed to take home. He'd reached in and gotten her coat, and she'd apologized for not bringing her things to the library as he had. "That's no problem, Liz. Let's grab a soda, go get my car and I'll take you home."

Her hesitation and blushing face surprised him. All the girls he had known before would've jumped at the chance to ride with any guy who had a car. He studied her face a little more closely and decided that this girl he'd just met today, who had welcomed him to the school and into her life, was a lot different from any other girl he'd ever met.

This is one girl I really want to check out thoroughly, in more ways than one, but I can't move too quickly. I don't want to scare her off. "Liz, I'm sorry. If your parents don't approve, or you're uncomfortable riding with me, I understand. After all, we just met this morning. I promise it would only be a ride home, but it's up to you. How will you get home otherwise?"

"I'll call my mom. Would you mind waiting just a minute?" After he'd nodded, she got out her cell phone and dialed. "Mom, I stayed after school to study Spanish with a new boy who just started to our school today. He has a car and has said he'll bring me home, but I wanted to check with you because I wasn't sure if I should accept a ride with him."

"I'll come and get you, Sweetie. See if he'll wait with you so I can meet him. We'll go from there."

"He's also mentioned coming to our house a couple of nights a week to study if it'd be O.K. with you and Dad, so you can decide if that would be all right, too. See you soon."

Turning back to Sergio, she said, "Mom would like to meet you if you can wait until she gets here."

"Sure, I'd be happy to do that, Liz. Let's hit the pop machine while we're waiting."

They talked to each other in Spanish for the few minutes they had to wait, and it was so much fun. They were laughing at their mistakes, mostly hers, but they decided it had gone quite well for the first try together.

Her mother arrived, met Sergio, asked some questions and then agreed that he could come to their house to study. "I'm impressed with the young man," she told Liz after they had gotten in the car and were driving home.

In class on Friday, Sergio and Liz sat next to each other again. The teacher was trying to pair the students up for study. Knowing that Liz would be good with a new student, she asked if the two of them would like to work on the assignment together. They agreed and then smiled at each other as if it had already been taken care of.

They'd planned to study again Saturday afternoon from 2:00 to 4:00. Toward the end of their studying, Sergio asked if she would like to go to a movie with him that evening.

"I'm sorry, Sergio, but I'm not allowed to date, unless chaperoned, until I'm 18. We could rent a movie and watch it here if you'd like."

Hesitating for a minute while he tried to digest

that bit of information, he finally said, "Okay, I'll go home pretty soon for dinner and get cleaned up. What time would you like me to come back?" He couldn't believe he'd just agreed to spend an evening with an apparently over-protected sophomore. This wasn't what he wanted at all, but it might be fun to play along and see what he might be able to accomplish.

"Would about 7:30 be all right?" Liz replied.

"Sure, I'll be here." Shortly after 5 o'clock, however, Liz received a phone call from Sergio. "My mother just reminded me that our family has been invited out for dinner, so I won't be able to come over tonight. I'm sorry, Liz, but I'll see you in school Monday."

"That's fine, Sergio. Have a good evening." On her way to the kitchen to help her mother fix dinner, she couldn't help but smile. *Is your family really invited out for dinner tonight, Sergio, or was it the idea of spending an evening watching a movie, possibly with my family, a little below what your motives were? I'm watching you closely, Mr. Silvano, and this is the first questionable act on your part. Will there be more?*

Chapter Eighteen

Arriving back at school a little later than he had originally planned, Josh discovered that the Registrar office had closed for the day. He'd have to wait until morning to add the Bible class to his schedule. He got his room organized and then decided to walk around the campus to see if he could find anyone he knew. It was a sunny day with only one or two big white clouds in the sky and a nice gentle breeze. He realized he was glad to be back and he'd found a few other early-birds to talk to. After strolling for over an hour, he just happened to notice the campus chapel. He'd never paid any attention to it before and he couldn't believe that he had never been inside. *It might be a good idea to check it out so I won't feel quite so out of place when I arrive there this Sunday.*

It was a very impressive sanctuary with a choir loft behind a raised dais, and padded pews which looked very inviting. He'd apparently walked farther than he'd realized because the pew felt quite good when he sat down. As he scanned the room, he observed the banners, the sconces with electric candles adorning the side walls, and the Christian and American flags at the front. As he dropped his eyes back to pew level, he found himself looking into the gorgeous green eyes of a very pretty redhead. She was staring at him so he smiled and acknowledged her presence, but she was then beside him almost immediately.

"You're Josh Holcomb, aren't you? I used to watch you practicing with the football team and wondered why you weren't in uniform on game days. I didn't see you at all this year. I'm April Higgins, and I like to come to the chapel occasionally so I can tell my mom I've been to church. I'm not much into this Jesus thing, but my parents worry less about me if they think I'm also learning something about God while attending college. Boy, would they be surprised if they really knew how I spend my time.

Are you a typical football player? Of course you are, or you wouldn't have been on the field. Would you like to spend the night with me? I have an apartment off campus with a really, really great bed. We could get a sandwich, since it's getting about that time, and then go have some fun. There aren't too many handsome guys back yet so it's a little dead around here today. You look like you're in good shape, so how about it?"

Josh was so shocked that he just sat there speechless. He couldn't think of a thing to say, but he was certainly wondering what was happening here and who was this girl? She was still watching him, as if expecting an answer, so he finally stammered, "I'm so sorry, April, but I'm not looking for that kind of an evening. I just came in to familiarize myself with the chapel so I wouldn't feel so out of place when I come Sunday. I'm ashamed that I haven't come my first three years, but I mean to be here as much as possible during my last semester. I'm a little surprised, though, that you don't want to learn about Jesus and His love for us no matter who or what we are. Although it wasn't too long ago, I can say that it's the most wonderful thing that's happened in my life so far." He then stood. "I guess I'd better go now, but maybe I'll see you here Sunday. It was certainly nice meeting you, April."

As they headed toward the door, she was glaring at him. "Don't look for me here, Mr. Goody Good Shoes. I should've known there was something wrong with you when you didn't really play in the games. You must be one of those little mommy's boys or you would have accepted my offer, but there are plenty of real men around so I'm never lonely."

Josh stood watching as she stomped off, but he couldn't get the grin off his face. *I've probably just been stamped as the small town boy who needs some big city training. It was different, I must say, and I know Jon will never believe it, but I do sort of wonder what she would've taught me.*

He couldn't help but chuckle as he stood pondering if he'd said the right things, but then a young man came out of the chapel and also stood watching April.

"I see you've met our April," he said with a smile. "She comes here more often than she'd care to admit. I'm afraid she's searching for God's love but settling for the human kind that has no lasting satisfaction or commitment. I heard what you said to her, Josh. I believe that's what she called you, and I'm so glad that you now have a good relationship with God. I'll be looking forward to seeing you here Sunday." He extended his hand as he said, "I'm Pastor Behrens." He then turned and went back inside the chapel.

Was I dreaming or did I just experience all this? Josh's thoughts were puzzling as he walked back to the dorm. *Maybe this semester is going to be rather interesting after all. I just need to get out and see what's going on a little more.* He then thought of Liz and tried to imagine her doing that little scene, but he couldn't keep from laughing out loud. He slowly reached over and touched the bracelet and immediately felt her presence beside him. *Can't I ever get you out of my thoughts, Princess?*

He noticed that the sun was going down now and the big red ball of fire was filtering through the now leafless trees on the quad. It was quite a sight to see, but it also made him a little homesick for the farm. He thought of the many times he'd been out riding and had been mesmerized by the sunset.

When he'd reached his Tahoe, his stomach was informing him that he hadn't eaten since he'd left home this morning, so he headed toward his favorite fast food restaurant in town. He was starving so he ordered two burgers, two orders of fries, and a chocolate malt. He drove around while finishing his malt and then stopped at a drug store to get some tooth paste that he realized he'd forgotten when he was unpacking earlier.

As he approached his room, he thought about the students coming back tomorrow and how the campus would then come alive. He spent the evening reviewing his test papers that he'd taken before going home for the holidays. He was hoping they would give him an idea of what the final tests might include. He already had more than enough credits to graduate, but he certainly wanted to pass these next tests even though he'd planned to stay and finish the year just for the extra knowledge he could acquire, especially now in Bible study.

Wednesday had passed rather quickly as he'd studied his schedule, registered for the additional class, and greeted some of the returning classmates. Now it was Thursday and his last few months of schooling were back in full swing.

∾

The professors had given Josh enough assignments to keep him busy all weekend, but he took time out to go watch the basketball game. He'd heard that they were pretty good this year in their division, and they proved that to be true. They'd played a great game.

Sunday morning he got up early, showered and dressed for church. When he walked into the lounge, a few of his friends started teasing him about being up and ready to go some place so early on a Sunday morning. He retorted with a smile. "I'm a changed man and I'm going to church this morning. Anyone want to join me?"

They all shook their heads and looked unbelievingly at him. One remarked, "More power to you if that's what you want to do while you're in college. As for me, I'm gonna sit right here and probably fall back asleep."

"You're missing out on a great relationship with

Jesus," he said with a smile and a wave. When he reached the chapel, he slipped into a pew about six rows from the back and was glancing around the sanctuary to see if he could see anyone he knew. The beautiful girl with the auburn hair and hazel eyes, whom he had seen in the Bible class Friday, was sitting about three rows in front of him. He was studying her profile as she talked to the girl next to her, but then he sensed someone sitting down beside him. He turned around to greet whoever it was, but then gasped, "April?"

April smiled at him and whispered, "You got my curiosity up the other day about this Jesus loving us, no matter what we've done. I decided to come and find out for myself if you were really telling me the truth. Do you mind if I sit here with you? I'll move if my being here makes you uncomfortable."

"No, I don't mind at all. I was just surprised to see you here after your remarks to me on Tuesday. How are your classes going?"

"Oh, they're OK. I'm studying to be a nurse so I enjoy all the classes pertaining to the care of patients. I hadn't realized we have so many parts that can go bad or get hurt before I started this course, but it's great to learn how many of them can also be fixed or cured."

The organ started playing the Prelude and they

both settled back to try to enjoy the service. It was outstanding with the college choir singing, the congregational songs, and the pastor's message which was right on target, Josh thought, for what April should be hearing. He was thinking about asking her to go to lunch, but she excused herself and headed down to the front of the chapel as soon as the service was over. Josh watched as she approached Dr. Behrens, talked to him for just a couple of minutes, and saw him nod affirmatively. It was then that Josh turned and left the chapel with his curiosity peaked as to what April was up to now. He actually surprised himself by whispering a little prayer asking that she be on the right path to learn of God's love and forgiveness.

Monday brought another unexpected situation Josh's way. When he entered the Bible class a little early, he noticed that the auburn beauty was there, too. She looked up and, when she saw him, she smiled and motioned for him to come over to her desk. "Hi, Josh, I just learned your name from the roster. I'm Melanie Grant, and I happened to see you sitting with April yesterday in chapel. I've been trying to find a way to get acquainted with her so I could invite her to some of the more informal meetings at the chapel, but I haven't had any luck. I wondered if you knew her well enough to introduce us."

"I only ran into her the other day when I was

checking out the chapel. She told me she didn't have much to do with this Jesus stuff and only came to the chapel so she could tell her folks she went to church. I was stunned when I saw her come in yesterday. She just said that my words had stirred up her curiosity, and she came to find out if I was telling the truth. I watched her talk to Dr. Behrens after chapel, but I have no idea what that was about."

"Well, you did more with one conversation than the rest of us have done during the past two years. Maybe we could talk to Dr. Behrens and see what's up. I've actually been helping him contact some students who have been brought to his attention either from their parents, other students or professors. Would you like to join us in this outreach?"

"Gosh, Melanie, I joined the class to learn more myself since I'd been sort of a rebel growing up, not listening to the pleas from my family, and thinking I knew it all. I recently got involved helping with an accident on my way home for the holidays that has changed my whole way of thinking, but I'm pretty new at all this."

"Maybe that's what some of the students need, someone who has been in their shoes and can understand their way of thinking. I'd really appreciate it if you would think about it, even if only for a month or two. You can let me know." Smiling, she asked,

"Are you dating someone who wouldn't want you doing this type of thing?"

"No, it's nothing like that. Let me think about it and I'll talk to you tomorrow."

After talking to Jon that night and then going to the chapel and having a conversation with Pastor Behrens, Josh decided to join the outreach program because it intrigued him. He thought it would be a way to meet some of the students he didn't yet know, and also a way to help him grow as a Christian.

He and Melanie spent a lot of time together, over the next few weeks, checking out their contacts, meeting with Pastor Behrens, and even relaxing at a movie. Josh actually felt that God might be leading him into a relationship with Melanie. He certainly did enjoy being with her and they had a similar background. Even though those vibes weren't there that he'd felt with Liz, who still invades his thoughts and dreams every day, he has begun to think that Melanie could be God's choice for his future. Since Liz has a new boyfriend, why wouldn't a new girl and a new direction for his life be in order?

Chapter Nineteen

It was finally Tuesday, February 14th, and Josh had been waiting all day for this very moment. It was Liz's 17th birthday and he had to call her before the family took off for the big shindig at the Country Club. He had been working with Melanie for over a month and he was getting to feel pretty close to her, but this was Liz's day and he had to let her know he was thinking of her, too. He had tried to figure out some way of crashing the party, but his schedule just wouldn't allow it. It was probably time to put this phase of his life behind him.

He realized his hand was shaking a little as he dialed, but he had only talked to Liz twice since he had returned to school and started spending time with Melanie. He didn't want to mention that tonight in case it might upset her. Liz had told him she had met a new boy at school and they were studying Spanish together, but he hadn't been able to bring himself to tell her about Melanie. He felt guilty about that, and he would have to tell her soon, just not tonight.

The phone kept ringing and he began to wonder if he had waited too long, but then he heard her sweet little voice, "Hello, this is the Becker residence, Liz speaking." He'd found himself speechless for a moment as his heart just wouldn't calm down, but he finally was able to say, "Happy Birthday, Sweet Princess. How is my precious little pipsqueak?"

"Oh, Josh, it's so nice of you to call. It seems like ages since we talked, but I've been so busy preparing for the trip to Spain and studying with Sergio. I do feel ashamed, but I haven't had time to really think. How are you doing?"

"I'm fine. My schedule has kept me hopping, too. I think I mentioned, the last time we talked, that I'm working with the pastor here at the campus chapel. I've been visiting with some of the students, sort of checking out their thoughts on attending church services and if they believe in God. That is, at times, one big headache. But, this is your birthday and you have a great big party to enjoy. Are you excited?"

"Yes, it's going to be fun. There will be about 25 friends and relatives there. I wish you could've made it. I got a package from you today and I'm so anxious to open it. I still wear the locket every day, and I'll be sure to think of you when I open this gift, whatever it is this time."

"Liz, why don't you open it now while I'm on the phone? I really don't want you to open it in front of everyone, because I'm sure it will mean a lot more to you if you see it in the privacy of your own room. That way you can concentrate on what it all stands for."

"Oh, Josh, may I? You really have my curiosity aroused now! It's right over here on my dresser so let me get it." She put the phone down but was back in an instant.

"Okay, I'm back. I had already taken the shipping paper off, but now I'm taking the pretty birthday paper off. The box is so pretty, Josh, but now I'm opening it. I'm lifting the cotton from over the top and........Oh, Josh, it's beautiful. It's a charm bracelet. And look at all the little charms!!! Oh, there's a princess, a bucking horse, which I really would rather *not* remember, and oooh, a little truck. Where did you find all these? Here's a tennis player, and oh, Josh, the dancing couple is so cute. And now I see a tiny locket and I think last, but not least, a heart. Oh, Josh, I'll treasure it forever. How were you able to find all those items that will always be memories of what we did together? I'm really in awe!"

"I'm glad you like it, Sweetheart. It took some time, but I had a lot of fun while I was searching for all the charms and, of course, thinking of you every step of the way. However, you mentioned not wanting to remember the bucking horse, but you do remember it was that horse that caused us to become good friends, don't you? When you were sitting by my bed when I awoke from that coma, I couldn't believe it was really you. Of course, you're still not telling me if you kissed me that day to wake me up, are you?"

"No, Josh, I'll never forget you being in the hospital because of that horse, but it was a miracle that we could become friends after the way we first got acquainted. You were such an impossible tease. I'm not going to give you the satisfaction of knowing whether I was the one who kissed you, either."

"O.K., I'll wait. You'll break down and tell me some day, and you just gave a pretty good hint that I *did* receive a kiss," he chuckled. "When do you leave for the Club?"

"I think they want to leave in about 15 minutes, but I'm all dressed and ready."

"That's good. It wouldn't be very smart to be running late if you got a zipper caught and I wasn't there to fix it for you," he chuckled. "Who all is coming from Hayes?"

"You're not going to let me forget that zipper,

210

are you? Coming from Hayes will be Christy and Jon as well as Grandpa and Grandma, Uncle Joseph and Aunt Marge, and also Brent and Susan. I invited about 12 friends from school including Sergio, whom I've told you about. Oh, Josh, he is so nice, and we are having a great time with our Spanish."

"Have you gotten the details about the trip yet, like when you leave, get back, etc.?"

"Yes, we'll leave on Saturday, the 18th of March, I'll join Mom and Dad in Paris on the 26th, and we'll fly home on April 1st or 2nd. Doesn't it sound fabulous?"

"Is your Sergio going to be on the trip, too?"

"Yes, he is. We've been practicing really hard so we'll be able to speak Spanish the entire week. It has helped a lot. I'm beginning to realize how right you were that I needed to enjoy my high school years. I hope you're having a good time in college this year, too. The work with the pastor sounds very rewarding."

There was no answer, so after a few moments of silence, she asked, "Josh, you've gotten awfully quiet---did I say something wrong?"

"No, Princess. I'm just remembering the good times we had together and getting a bit sentimental, I guess. I'd better let you go so you won't be late for your 17th birthday party. Please tell the gang from Hayes and your family I said 'hello'. Oh, Liz, have you had your first kiss today, now that you're one year older?"

"No, Josh, I haven't, but I doubt if it'll be too much longer. Sergio has been hinting that he would like to finally get a kiss on my birthday. He's remarked quite often that he thinks I'm over protected by my parents, but he hasn't been quite as bold as you were. Maybe I was the bold one with you, but I always felt so safe for some reason," she giggled.

"I'm glad you've waited, Princess. I always realized just how young you were, and I wanted to be your protector. I probably wasn't the best one around, but I certainly enjoyed those kisses we shared, and I still remember them in my dreams. And, your Sergio doesn't get the first one today. Put your lips to the phone, Sweetheart, because a big 17th birthday kiss is coming through." All the sounds of a big, sloppy kiss came across the lines and then landed on her lips that she had pressed to the ear piece.

"Thank you so much, Josh. You will always be my knight in shining armor. I'll love you forever, in a special way, but I'd better go because my young prince is now waiting for me." Giggling again, she said, "Bye, Josh," and then she was gone.

Well, I guess it's my own fault that I've lost my princess, Josh thought to himself. *It sounds like she is really taken with this Sergio, so I pray that he will be exactly what she wants and needs. Now, I hope I can get on with my life with no backward glances or regrets, but I'm not sure I'll ever be able to forget my princess or keep her out of my dreams..*

He called Melanie to tell her he was on his way, took her the pretty valentine he'd bought earlier that day, and stopped on the way to pick up a long-stemmed rose in a vase with a red ribbon tied around it. He really did enjoy the rest of the evening, although he occasionally had a thought pop into his head about the birthday party going on in Colorado Springs.

On Sunday, he called Jon to see how things were going. Of course, he had to hear all about Liz's party, and it must've been a blast, ending with the whole group going outside to take a look at the car her parents had bought for her. She had been speechless, but thrilled.

∽

Josh and Melanie became more and more involved with the pastor. He'd confided in them that he had been meeting with April twice a week for Christian studies, she had been baptized and she was a completely changed person. "She is considering joining the Doctors without Borders and going wherever needed," the pastor remarked. "It was just an absolute miracle we saw here due to one conversation she had with you,

213

Josh. She told me you had really made her stop and think about what she was doing with her life."

"I'm glad that I helped although I can't remember what I could have said that made a deep impression like that."

"Sometimes I feel it is God who is talking through us, Josh, and we are just the ones he chooses for a particular situation. However it happened, April is so grateful, I am really thankful, and God must be very happy."

The following weeks were busy as he and Melanie became almost inseparable and he felt his life was going on the right track. Melanie had grown up on a farm and enjoyed all the little things he did. She was studying to be a teacher and he knew she'd be a good one. It was just a matter of time now, he thought, until he asked if there could be a future for the two of them. It seemed like such a short time ago that he hadn't wanted a romantic relationship with anyone because of his schooling and then learning all the facets of the farm still ahead. His precious Liz had changed that feeling and he was now ready to start considering having a wife in the near future. A few things were missing in this relationship that he'd loved with Liz, but he thought that was to be expected. Those exciting tingles and feelings he'd had with Liz, even when on the phone, don't seem to be there with Melanie, and he also misses the teasing that he'd loved so much with Liz because of her cute reactions. Melanie is a very serious person so teasing is most likely going to be out of line, but he feels he can get along without that since he probably needs to grow up anyway.

Two weeks before Spring Break, Melanie asked Josh if he'd like to join a group that is going from the college to spend the week of their break helping along the Gulf coast still recovering from the hurricane. He had readily agreed, but in his mind he was picturing Liz enjoying beautiful Barcelona, Spain and Paris, France while he was doing backbreaking work to help people recover from a disaster. He rather envied her the trip, but he felt that what he would be doing was God's plan for him right now, and he was looking forward to it.

On March 16th, he called to wish Liz a bon voyage and hoped it would be a trip that she would never forget. He told her what he would be doing, and she wished him God's guidance and protection. She told him she'd be praying for him and he dittoed the thought for her. It was hard for either of them to say goodbye, but finally Liz started singing a little ditty, "Goodnight, My Friend, Goodnight, My Friend, May God watch over you."

Josh replied in his deep bass, "Goodbye, My Dear,

Goodbye to You, but My Love will always be true." They were both still laughing when they clicked off, but Josh couldn't shake the feeling that something wasn't quite right about this trip of hers. Maybe it was because he was wishing he was going with her, but he still promised that all his prayers would include a plea for the safety of Liz.

✎

Liz could hardly sleep Friday night knowing she would be on a plane to Spain in the morning. When she and Sergio had been assigned seats next to each other, she had been so excited. She got to thinking, however, how different her feelings were toward Sergio from the ones she'd felt with Josh. She was especially surprised that she hadn't had any of the vibes or those tingling feelings around Sergio that she'd felt when she'd been with Josh, even when she had talked to him on the phone Thursday night. She'd decided, however, she'd not linger on that thought. After all, Sergio isn't as old or maybe as experienced as Josh, and perhaps the age difference had been what had excited her about Josh.

"I am so happy," she chanted as she danced around the room, "and during one of our recent talks, Josh told me that he was dating a wonderful girl. Everything's working out fine, but I still miss him so much. I just pray that God will be there for both of us."

The flight was a long one, and they were given most of Sunday, with the time change, to get over their jet lag. She and her room mate did a lot of talking in Spanish and English, and they learned that both had boyfriends on the trip that they would be spending a lot of time with, and the week went by pretty fast. On Monday, they strolled along La Rambla, the most famous street in Barcelona which leads down to the Mediterranean Sea. It was filled with pedestrians and lined with outdoor markets, shops, restaurants, and cafes. It had been great fun speaking to the clerks, waiters, and some people on the street in Spanish, and then watching them smile when they realized they were Americans.

Tuesday they toured the Picasso Museum where the collection is displayed in three adjoining medieval palaces. Picasso had started his long artistic career in Barcelona.

On Wednesday the chaperones had planned a trip to Tibidabo Mountain, the oldest and only remaining amusement park in Spain. It had been built in 1899 and had 30 exciting rides. Fantastic views of the city could be seen from the Watch Tower and the Ferris wheel.

Thursday was either a trip to the L'Aquarium de

Barcelona, an ultra modern aquarium and one of the biggest in Europe, and it has the best collection of Mediterranean marine life, or a park which was made totally of ceramic tile forms.

On Friday the whole group went to Sagrada Familia, the most famous landmark in Barcelona. It had been started in 1882 by Antoni Gaudi, but he died in 1926 before it had been completed. Just to stroll around the perimeter of the structure was amazing as you saw the remarkable decorations adorning the spires and facade. Inside there is only scaffolding and unfinished work although, for a fee, you can be raised to the top from where you can see another spectacular view of the city.

When they'd returned from Sagrada Familia, they'd had some free time. Liz had noticed that Sergio became a little moody when they stopped to get a cold drink. "Is there something wrong?" she asked.

He just looked at her with a look of disgust. "I really thought, Liz, that when you got away from home and your tight-armed family, you'd at least be a little more romantic toward me. I haven't had a single kiss the whole week and no time alone like I'd hoped."

"What do you mean, Sergio? We've spent almost all the time together and I've really enjoyed being with you. I've just loved the experience of being in Spain.

There wasn't much time or a place to do much kissing, I realize, but we'll be able to do that back home."

"If you've enjoyed it so much, let me come to your room tonight. You *are* 17 now, you know, and most girls, by the time they're your age, are ready to find out what sex is all about, if they haven't already. So, will you be with me tonight, Liz? I think I've been pretty patient since we met well over two months ago."

Liz gasped and knew she was turning beet red. She could only remember the times she'd spent with Josh and how protective he'd been of her. Luckily, she and Sergio were alone in the booth so nobody else was around to hear this rift. She just stared at him, terribly shocked and stupefied. "Did I hear you correctly, Sergio?" she whispered when she was able to finally open her mouth to speak. "You honestly want me to let you come to my room here in Barcelona and have sex tonight?"

"It's no big deal, Liz. Everybody does it. I didn't push it before because I realized you were more innocent that most girls I've known. But this trip is an ideal time for you to find out what goes on between a boy and a girl when they like each other. It doesn't mean that we'll be going steady or anything."

"I thought I had gotten to know you, Sergio, but I see that I was so very wrong. You don't know *me*, that's for sure, so I'll tell you a thing or two. The first is that I do not have a private room, but it wouldn't matter if I did, because you would *not* be invited there. The second is that I am a Christian, my life is in God's hands, and I have no intention of having sex with you or any other male until I'm married. We've had a nice time together preparing for the trip and enjoying this week, but it is ending here and now. Goodbye, Sergio."

She quickly grabbed her purse, but on her way out of the booth she picked up the rest of her drink and threw it in his face. She was out the door before he could respond, but she returned to her room and fell on the bed in tears. Where had she gone wrong?

When her roommate, a senior, returned and found Liz crying, they had a long talk and learned that both of them had given their lives to Christ. "I'm sorry you had to face that, Liz, but now you know what a lot of boys expect even if you've spent very little time with them. I imagine Sergio will be much more careful if and when he approaches another girl in this school unless he likes cold drinks in his face. Most of us are *not* party girls," she giggled.

That evening, after dinner, the whole group went to the Font Magica de Montjuic, a water fountain, built in 1929, which combines music, light, and changing forms of water to create a spectacular display. The fountains dance for 30 minutes to a variety of music, and there are several different shows. Liz enjoyed the evening with her roommate, whose boyfriend was spending the evening with the guys, and some of the other girls. Liz didn't much care how Sergio was spending his.

Chapter Twenty

With their classes finished Friday afternoon, the 17th, Josh and Melanie were on their way with about 22 other students, plus two professors, who had boarded the bus. They were headed south to work in Louisiana. They'd been told it would probably be dark when they got to their destination, and then they'd have to pitch the two big tents before they could get some rest. So, after they'd stopped for something to eat, most decided it was a good time to catch a little shuteye.

About 7 a.m. the next morning and each following day, they were given assignments that were hard work and long hours, but the week proved to be very satisfying. They were able to see quite a difference by the time they left the next Saturday afternoon. Actually, Josh and Melanie had seen very little of each other, but they were so glad they had gone to help. Although they were sore, dirty, and very tired, it had been a great experience. When it was over and they'd returned to campus, they needed all day Sunday to recuperate to be ready for classes on Monday.

Monday and Tuesday evenings were spent just milling around the campus, going into town to do some shopping and then taking in a movie Tuesday night. When they'd reached her residence hall, Josh shut off the motor and pulled her over into his arms. "You know, Melanie, I feel we've gotten very close over the last three months. We're both going to be graduating soon, so I was wondering if you might be ready and willing to make a lifetime commitment with me. I've become very fond of you, as you probably already know, our interests are the same, our beliefs are the same, and our kisses have a lot of potential," he chuckled. "I feel we could have a very good life together. What do you think?" He'd leaned down to give her a kiss, but she'd quickly pulled away. He gave her a surprised look because she'd always responded enthusiastically to his kisses before. "Did I do something wrong, Melanie? I thought you'd enjoyed our kisses."

"I'm sorry, Josh, it wasn't the kiss; but my plans right now do not include marriage. I *might* be ready in two or three years, but I want to teach and I don't want to be tied down in one place with a husband possibly wanting a family. I've always wanted to be a teacher who could select the area of the country where she would teach, travel during the summers, and do my own thing. It just doesn't fit my plan to think of marriage so soon after graduation. A lot of young people are not getting married until they're in their thirties, and that also appeals to me. I certainly didn't mean to give you any false impression. I thought we were just very good friends working in the out-reach program and enjoying each other's company. I'm sorry if you took it any other way."

"Thanks for clarifying that for me, Melanie. I guess I have some adjustments to make in my plans for the future. I think maybe we should call it a night now, don't you?" He went around to open the door for her, and then walked silently beside her just to the entrance of the building. He gave her a quick kiss, actually on the cheek, and then turned facing his car. He muttered "Goodnight, Melanie," as he walked away. *Or is it Goodbye?*

When he reached his room, he hardly had the strength left to stand up, so he lay down on the bed, stared at the ceiling, and felt the tears trying to fall off his lashes. *You want me to wait two or three years and then possibly find that you want to teach a few more years before you finally decide it's time to get married? I'm just glad I hadn't bought you a ring. I could have had my Precious Princess by that time. Oh, Liz, what did I do? Didn't I listen to God closely enough? I pushed you away, because I really felt you needed your high school years. That has been proven correct, I guess, with your chance to go to Spain and all. But now you are out of my life and I'm completely alone."* He just lay there and sobbed until he finally fell asleep, still fully dressed.

It wasn't yet 6 o'clock the next morning when Josh awoke to his cell phone's crazy ring. He mumbled to himself, "I don't need any more explanations, Melanie. I heard you loud and clear last night." He dragged himself to the desk, however, and fumbled around until he found his phone hidden under some papers. "Hello, this had better be good," he barked.

"Josh, I'm sorry if I woke you, but this is a dire emergency. Are you all right?" Jon's voice really sounded concerned and Josh was now wide awake. He glanced at his wrinkled clothes and softly moaned.

"I'm sorry, Jon, I thought it might be someone else. What's wrong? You sound as if something really bad has happened."

"Well, it has, and we need your help if you can get away from school. I know you've had all your exams and just got back from spring break a few days ago, but we may need you longer than just a few days.

They rushed Christy's dad to the hospital in Pueblo last evening, most likely the dreaded heart attack. Almost immediately, they airlifted him from there up to Colorado Springs. They'd contacted Denver, but were told that the best heart specialist in the area, and the closest for us, was in Colorado Springs. I could hardly believe it when they told us it was Dr. Dan Wilder. He's been there throughout the night, and it doesn't look too good right now. The whole family is worried sick, of course.

Brent wants to stay at the hospital with his mom and Christy, but he's also concerned about the ranch. He has talked to the hired hands and they'll handle the morning chores, but he doesn't feel they can do it for any length of time without some supervision. I mentioned that I could call you, and he would be so appreciative if you could come manage the ranch until they know for sure what the situation is with Joseph. The rest of the week may be all we'll need, but it would be great if you could plan on staying a little longer. I know we're asking a lot of you to leave school when you'd wanted to finish the year, but you're the only one I knew who could possibly do the job."

"Give me an hour to get my things loaded and I'll be out of here. Do you want me to go directly to the ranch or stop at the office first?"

"Why don't you stop at the office and we'll talk

to Noah. He's been at the hospital, of course, but he's coming back this morning for a couple appointments. He'll be able to tell you more about the daily routine at the ranch, and we'll go from there."

"I appreciate your confidence in me, Jon, and I'll be on my way shortly." While he'd been talking to Jon, he'd been packing, so he was on his way in less than the hour.

Josh thought he should call Melanie so she wouldn't think he'd run off because of her remarks last night, but he decided it was too early. He'd call her later while on the road. He wanted to put the accelerator to the floor, but remembered the accident he had witnessed and held it to the legal speed. It was a good 7 or 8 hour drive, and his mind was drifting from one thing to another.

He wondered if Jon had called their dad and mom. He was sure they would be awake so he dialed and waited. His mom answered, and he told her all he knew about the situation because Jon hadn't called them yet. She was so glad he was available to help, and of course, had to remind him to be careful driving.

He called Melanie about 8:30 and told her he wasn't sure if he would be returning to school. He would try to make it for graduation, but that would depend on how things went at the ranch. After clicking off, he mumbled, "Goodbye, Melanie, it was nice while it lasted." He was surprised he didn't feel too sorry about this break-up, but he sure hated losing Liz.

❧

Liz was feeling like she never wanted to see Colorado Springs, her school, or to face Sergio again. She'd avoided him Friday night at the fountain, and also on Saturday by sticking close to her roommate and some of the other girls who wanted to go strolling down the La Ramble again and to the zoo. A meeting had been called for late afternoon at which time the teacher discussed the departing plans for tomorrow. Liz was told that one of the chaperones would see that she got to her plane because she was scheduled to leave before the rest of the group. A final dinner was served for them in a private room of the hotel, but Liz again was able to find a seat with the girls. She didn't even try to see where Sergio was sitting or if he was even there.

When she'd arrived in Paris, her parents immediately knew that something was wrong but she wouldn't discuss it with them. The few days in France, with several side trips, were interesting, but she was too upset to enjoy them as she'd anticipated. She could only think of Josh's birthday on April 1st, and she wasn't going to be there to talk to him. *I'll make it up to him someway, but it probably won't matter to him since he has that Melanie to hug and kiss. Oh, why is growing up such a pain?*

After they'd been notified that Joseph was in the hospital, Liz and her parents flew home on Thursday, the 30th. Then, when Liz learned that Josh had come up to manage the ranch so Brent could be with Aunt Marge and Christy, she rushed to her room and tried to calm her nerves. Her mind was going at full speed as she was pacing the floor and trying to figure out what to do. *Josh is at the ranch and I have to see him, but how can I get down there? If my parents will let me drive that far by myself, it'll be a miracle, but I have to try.*

She decided to talk to her dad first because she had always been able to convince him to let her do things easier than her mom. She found him in the library and after she'd cried a little and begged a lot, she was finally able to win him over. She could drive down to Hayes tomorrow and come back Sunday. He'd checked with Eleanor to see if it was OK and was assured that she and Noah would be thrilled to have her. They'd also keep a close eye on the happenings between her and Josh.

After baking and packing Friday morning, she's now on her way to the ranch with a birthday cake on the back seat and a birthday present beside it. She can hardly wait until she pulls into the drive, and then she sees Josh at the barn door. *I don't know how close he and this Melanie are, but I don't care. I have to talk to someone and the only one I want to talk to is Josh.*

Dr. Becker had called Josh after Liz was on the road early Friday afternoon. He told him of her despondency when she'd joined them in Paris, but that they hadn't been able to get her to talk about it. "So, when she insisted she had to talk to you, Josh, I couldn't refuse her. I felt maybe you could help where we had failed. I'm calling without her knowledge, but I wanted you forewarned that she's a very distraught young lady right now, so I'm asking you to please be gentle with her. OK?"

"Thanks, Dr. Becker, for the warning. I'll be very careful as I try my best to find out what is bothering the little princess, and thanks for letting her come to see me. That must've been a rather hard decision," he chuckled, "but I'll let you know what I find out, unless she forbids me to."

"I understand, Josh, and we'll respect the confidentiality she places in you. We only want her to be the sweet, trusting, and outgoing person she has always been."

Josh's mind was going in circles trying to imagine what had happened in Spain that would have her so upset. With chaperones and in a group like that, he didn't want to think of a problem Sergio could have caused her, but he was also remembering the feeling he'd had, the last time they'd talked, that something wasn't right about her trip. He was ready to attack a certain boy if he'd taken advantage of his princess, so he was rather worked up himself by the time he saw a small compact car pull into the drive. He didn't recognize it, but assumed it had to be the one Liz had gotten for her birthday.

He was standing at the door of the barn, and he watched as she jumped out of the car, almost before it was completely stopped, and came running into his arms. She started crying uncontrollably, and all he could do was hold her, kiss the top of her head, and whisper that it would all be OK. She'd finally calmed down, looked up at him and smiled. "That wasn't the best greeting I could've given you when we haven't seen each other for so long. Oh, Josh, I don't know where to begin, but life seems to have handed me a double whammy." She tried to wipe her eyes with the back of her hands and then took a deep gasp of air.

Josh pulled a handkerchief from his pocket and wiped the tears from her cheeks as he softly said, "Just take your time and get your breath, Princess. We have the rest of the day to talk and get to the bottom of what is bothering you. Take it at your own speed and tell me what has happened to make you feel so sad."

"It'll probably sound like nothing to you," she

swallowed hard, "since you're a man, but it completely ruined my trip. I was having so much fun, and it was wonderful being with Sergio most of the time. Then, on Friday," she said as she started to sob again, "he told me that he'd expected me to be more romantic toward him when I'd gotten away from my over-protective parents. He asked if I would let him come to my room that night, and then went on to tell me that almost everybody does it, and since I'm 17 now, I should want to find out what sex is all about. I was so stunned, upset, and so terribly disappointed in him, but I still had the courage to tell him I was a Christian and no boy, or man, was going to have sex with me until I was married. I even threw the rest of my drink in his face as I left him there and ran back to my room.

I avoided him Friday night and Saturday, and then I flew to meet my parents Sunday morning. I was never so humiliated in my life. I couldn't talk about it to Mom and Dad, but I know they realized something was wrong. I remembered your birthday was supposed to be the day we got back, and I was hoping I could call and talk to you, but now I'll get to be here for your birthday tomorrow. Josh, what am I going to do? I'd thought God was leading my life, but now I've lost you to *that Melanie* and I've lost Sergio, luckily I guess, but I feel like my life is a complete mess."

"Please just relax, Princess, because things aren't

as bad as they seem. The number one problem, which I think is the most important one for you to know the answer to right now, is that I am not lost to *that Melanie*," he chuckled. "She has informed me that she had just considered us very good friends and that she had no intentions of it being anything else for at least two, three or more years. The answer to the number two problem, that Sergio kid, is that he's the most stupid jerk in the country to think he could pull that on the wisest little princess in the whole world. Now, number three isn't a problem at all, but it is strictly up to you, Princess. If I have to wait for two or three years for the wife of my dreams, I'm going to wait for my Princess, if she'll have me, that is."

He very tenderly lifted her chin to look at those beautiful brown eyes and found them as big as saucers. She threw her arms around his neck and held on for dear life. "Are you sure, Josh? Has God actually brought us back together?" With a little giggle, she added, "I never did experience those unusual and exciting feelings with Sergio that I had with you. I remember you warned me to watch for them, but could they be something I'll only be lucky enough to experience with you?"

"I hope so." He then proceeded to answer more fully with one little kiss that sent tingles all over his body. "Oh, Lord, am I still on this planet?" he sighed

233

when he'd found his voice. "Now," he said as he held her away a few inches and grinned, "you'd better go check in with your grandmother. I imagine she's expecting you and is probably keeping her eagle eye on the two of us since your dad talked to her about your coming."

"Yes, Daddy said he called and got permission for me to stay with them, but how do you know about my grandmother's eagle eye after knowing her for such a short time?"

"I have two wonderful grandmothers, Princess, and I can spot those loving, but ever alert eyes with very little trouble."

"Oh, I guess a grandmother's love is precious but also makes you think about what you're doing so you won't get into trouble with her. I'll have to remember that. I brought a birthday cake for you. It's in the car with a small present. Can we have it later tonight?"

"You bet, Sweetie. Noah and Eleanor have been kind enough to feed me since I got here, so I'll be over in a little while. There are just a few more things to do to finish up for the day. It's been great getting to help out like this."

Liz took her things into the house, got settled in her room, and then helped Grandma fix the evening meal. She asked if it was all right to have the cake to celebrate both Josh and Grandpa's birthdays, even if it was a day early. She got a big hug and a nod since it had not even been considered after Joseph was taken to the hospital.

Noah came home, bringing Jon with him, because Christy was going to stay at the hospital again tonight. The enlarged dinner table thrilled Noah because he loved it whenever his family was together. When Josh joined them, Noah thought he sensed a little romance sprouting between Liz and Josh again although he couldn't be sure about the ending to this one, or his feelings about it. *It most likely wouldn't have been one that I, as Cupid, would've encouraged, but only time will tell. Cupid can't be right every time, but three out of four isn't too bad.* Of course, he was thinking of the romances and marriages of Joseph and Margaret and of Jon and Christy that he'd helped get off the ground. He is hoping now that Brent will make the move and ask Susan to be his wife. It's been over two years, and Noah feels that is long enough for a couple to decide if they're right for each other or not.

Right now, however, his mind shifted back to the current crisis in the family, his son's health. His prayer before dinner included a fervent prayer for healing, and for the safety of all members of the family who would be traveling and standing vigil in the days ahead.

Chapter Twenty-One

Everyone was concerned about Joseph and kept in close touch with the members of the family who were not leaving the hospital. Test after test had been taken but no definite decision had been made by the medical team. Dr. Wilder had informed them that one carotid artery was 85% blocked, but that didn't disturb him as much as the arteries around his heart cavity. He was trying to determine if Joseph was actually strong enough to undergo surgery with multiple by-passes. He'd asked quite a few questions about the last few months and also about Joseph's behavior such as tiredness, agitation, and breathlessness. Had anyone noticed him doing things differently than he would normally, and had he mentioned any pain?

Brent spoke up and told about his dad stopping

occasionally in the barn and taking a few deep breaths, but brushed it off when Brent had asked him about it. He had acted a little upset that Brent had even noticed. They'd all tried to think back but couldn't remember that he'd acted tired, nor had he gone to bed earlier than usual. If he was a little upset at times, he always handled it graciously. This just seemed to have hit him all at once.

Dr. Wilder thanked them for their input and said he would check back in just a little while, so they were surprised when he was back very quickly. He informed them that they were taking Joseph to surgery immediately as he'd had another light attack so they couldn't hold off any longer. The long vigil began.

The call to Noah and Eleanor came as they were finishing up their ice cream and cake to celebrate Noah and Josh's birthdays. Of course, Noah, Eleanor, and Jon all wanted to go to the hospital to be with the family, but then they looked at Liz and Josh.

Josh looked astonished, "Please, do you think I would take advantage of a situation as dire as this? We'll call Liz's folks, and if they don't want us to be here together, then I'll just follow her home or one of them can drive down here. Nothing is going to happen to Liz, I'll assure you."

Noah spoke up, "If you're anything like your brother, Josh, then I have all the faith in the world in you, but I do think we should let her parents make the decision. What do you think, Jon?"

"I'd trust my brother with my life, Noah, but I agree that David and Rachel should be informed about the situation here. They should definitely make the final decision."

Liz was already heading for the phone. Her dad answered quickly, and knowing she was calling about Joseph, informed her that Marge had called and that he and her mother were going to the hospital right away. Since they had also realized that Noah and Eleanor would also want to be there, they'd discussed the possibility and decided that Liz would be fine staying there with Josh. "You know the rules, Honey," her dad told her, "and you also know what the consequences can be if you don't follow them. Let me speak to Josh for just a moment, will you please?" Liz handed the phone to Josh.

"Yes, Dr. Becker, this is Josh."

"Josh, we are going out on a limb here, but I'm glad you're there to stay with Liz so the others can come to the hospital. It's a difficult time for the family and we're glad she has you to lean on. Did she happen to tell you anything?"

"Yes, and I want to assure you that everything will be fine. I cherish this precious daughter of yours, and I would do nothing to harm her. I appreciate your trust in me, Dr. Becker, and I accept with pleasure the responsibility to protect her while her family is gone. We'll both be praying for a successful surgery. I do hope you believe me."

"We do, Josh. In fact, we feel pretty lucky to have you in our corner."

Please give my best to Marge, Christy, and Brent, and I'll watch over the ranch and Liz for all of you."

"Thanks again, Josh, and a Happy Birthday tomorrow. Goodnight, now."

"Goodnight, Sir, and thank *you*."

After being assured that Josh and Liz would clean up the kitchen, Eleanor hastily put on some different clothes, got some extra clothes for Marge and Brent, and then the three of them were on their way.

Josh thought he and Liz were a great team as they worked to get the kitchen spic and span. He had helped Eleanor the last two nights, since he had been there, so he knew where some of the things went, but Liz was much more familiar with the kitchen, so she did most of the putting away. They'd had fun splashing some suds on each other and then Josh snapped her with the towel. She was actually laughing as she yelled, "Josh, you're mean, and I'll get you for that." She started chasing him around the room with the wet sponge in her hand, but when he decided to stop short, she had plowed right into his back. The sponge in her hand just happened to land in his hair as she'd been waving it in the air. He took the sponge and threw it into the sink and then pulled her into his arms.

"Now, what are you going to do, Little Lady? I've got you and I may not let you go for hours. What would you think about that?"

"Well, I may just kick you so hard in the leg that you'll be screaming with pain and let me go, or maybe I'll just decide to stay in your arms for all those hours until you get tired of holding me."

"You're dreaming, Princess, if you think I would ever tire of holding you, but right now I'd better let you go so we can finish our job here."

After the kitchen was all nice and clean, they started to watch a movie on TV, but it wasn't too interesting. They also realized that it was getting late and Josh had to be up early in the morning, too. Liz jumped up and dashed upstairs before he could even say goodnight, but she returned shortly carrying a small package. "It isn't much, Josh, but I wanted to bring you a little something from Paris. I'm glad it can still be considered a birthday present."

"You shouldn't have done that, Princess, but I sure appreciate your thinking about me while you were so far away." He opened it to find a French brand of after shave lotion, and it certainly did smell good.

"I don't think I can wear this around the barn and

stables, so I'll have to save it just for when I'm with you," he chuckled. "Let me give you just one little kiss as a thank you." Josh pulled her into his arms and was going to just kiss her cheek, but Liz had her arms around his neck and her lips on his mouth for a full-blown spine-tingling kiss. He could do nothing but respond until he gently pushed her away, gasping. "Princess, that is no way for you to stay safe, so you scoot yourself up to bed, now!"

"Have you decided where you're going to sleep?" she asked so demurely.

He wasn't quite sure what he should do as he had been staying at the main house, but he couldn't or wouldn't leave Liz alone here at Noah's either. Liz had informed him earlier that there were plenty of bedrooms upstairs, but he decided he'd better sleep on the couch and stay downstairs. When Liz was told that, she was soon back again with a pillow, a sheet and a blanket with which she made him a bed on the couch. He again headed her toward the stairs as he said, "Goodnight, Liz, sleep tight, and don't come down here again."

Josh had to admit that he was tired from the two full days' work on the ranch, a new experience from all his college days, but he was overly excited about the opportunity that had been given him. He loves this ranch, but most of all, he realized, he loves that little princess asleep in one of the bedrooms upstairs. He thought of how he had tried to walk away from her, tried to start another relationship, but now, somehow, they were back together. Liz had also tried and failed to find a new love, and had come to him for comfort and understanding. *It has to be God working these miracles, but first giving us a glimpse of how another person might affect our lives. Can it possibly be that our futures will find us together?* He'd finally fallen asleep and dreamed about the two of them being man and wife.

When Josh awoke the following morning, the first thing he noticed was the smell of sausage and coffee coming from the kitchen. He tossed the covers off, pulled his jeans and shirt on, and then grabbing his shoes and socks, he nearly ran to the kitchen. There she was, a big apron tied around her waist, breaking eggs into the skillet. He couldn't resist putting his arms around her waist and kissing her cheek as she turned toward him.

"I hope you like sausage and eggs, Josh," she smiled as she gently pushed him away, "but you're going to be in trouble with the hired hands if you don't start eating and get to your tasks. Brent is always out there bright and early." A plate of sausage, hash browns and eggs were placed on the table. Josh poured himself a cup of coffee and obediently sat down where she'd put the plate. She was back with toast, jelly, and orange juice.

"You must think you're feeding my brother because I don't usually eat this much. I'll be so full I won't be able to do the chores. But, where is yours?"

"I'm coming with mine, but you get started right now so you can get to work."

"Are you always this bossy when you're the cook?" he chuckled.

"I don't know since I haven't been in this position before," she giggled as she sat down with a glass of orange juice and a piece of toast.

"Is that all you're going to eat? That isn't enough to keep a bird alive."

"I'm sorry, Josh, if I sound bossy. I'm just concerned, want you to do well and be well fed because this is a whole new experience for you, too. You aren't a schoolboy any more, so maybe you need someone to boss you a little," she grinned. "You have a full day of hard work ahead of you so you need a good breakfast."

"I've lived on a farm all my life, Liz, so I'm not completely out of my element here. Will you eat some of this on my plate?"

I'll take a bite or two if you think I fixed you too much." She smiled as she reached over and picked up a small piece of sausage daintily with her fingers and

243

put it in her mouth. She then reached for a piece of scrambled egg.

Josh couldn't help laughing. "You are something else, Princess. What are you going to do today to keep yourself busy?"

"I'm going to pretend that I'm Eleanor and do my wifely chores. I have the dishes to wash, beds to make, and check the kitchen floor to make sure no food was dropped. Grandma always does that because she says Grandpa is getting a little sloppy as he eats." She giggled as she went and got the coffee pot to pour him another cup of coffee.

"You'll make someone a wonderful wife someday, Liz. Are you going to do anything fun like maybe go into town or go riding? I should have some time this afternoon if you'd like to go riding or play some tennis. The sun is shining so it probably won't be too cold. It's also April and that means Spring is here and some flowers may be showing up on the trails."

"I thought I would go to the main house and see if anything needs to be done there, and then I'll come back, read my devotions, and fix your lunch. You can come in for lunch, can't you? I'll know by then what I want to do this afternoon."

"I'll be here, if that's what you want to do, but I hate to see you spending your whole weekend doing housework. Of course, you just had a get-away-trip to

Spain and France so maybe you're ready to do some daily chores around home," he chuckled.

"I think I mentioned to you once before that I don't want a college education. I just want to be a wife and mother. This is wonderful training, especially when I'm doing it for you." she grinned.

"Liz, you're still too young to know for sure what you want to do with the rest of your life. I know God has given us time together again, after we've both had disappointments, but that doesn't mean there aren't more experiences coming that may change our futures."

"Josh Holcomb, I'm going to ignore that remark because I simply don't agree. You go to work now and think about what has happened in the last two weeks. As for me, I'm going to accept the fact that God *has* given us this opportunity to be together again. After showing me what other guys are always thinking about and expecting, I realize now just how lucky I was to find you. I know I didn't think that when I first met you because you were such a big tease, but I've learned what a great person you really are, and I'm actually beginning to like your teasing."

"You certainly know how to give my ego a boost, Sweetie, but I'd better be on my way now." Giving her a quick kiss on the cheek, he hurried out the door, but he couldn't keep from smiling at the antics and the confession of that sweet little seventeen-year-old about what she wants in her future. He's also decided he'd love to have her for his wife one day, but it's way too soon to tell *her* that. She has two years of high school left, and he's going to do his best to make sure she has that diploma and the memorable experiences that go along with high school days.

Chapter Twenty-Two

The phone was ringing when Liz returned from the main house where she'd gone to see that the beds were made and the kitchen was clean. She didn't know exactly when it was that they'd left for the hospital with Joseph so she wanted everything to be in order when they came back. She also made sure the bread was fresh and everything was fresh in the fridge in case Josh got hungry between the meals he had with Grandpa and Grandma. But now she dashed to answer the phone and found Grandma calling from the hospital. "Grandma, I'm so glad to hear from you. How did the surgery go last night, and is Uncle Joseph going to be OK?"

"Well, Dear, the surgery is over, but it was a long and difficult procedure from what we've been told.

Joseph is in the ICU now and being watched very carefully. Only one at a time can go in and that is for 5 minutes and only once an hour. He is far from being out of danger, and we all need to pray diligently. Marge, of course, will not leave the hospital and Brent insists on staying with her, but the rest of us are coming home tonight. Jon persuaded Christy to come home and get a good night's rest and then they'll both come back up here tomorrow. So, how have you and Josh been?"

"Oh, we're fine. We finished cleaning the kitchen after you left and then we started to watch a movie on TV. It wasn't very interesting and it was getting late, so I ran upstairs and got the gift I'd bought for him in Paris. After opening it and telling me he couldn't wear that wonderful smell in the barn so he'd save it to wear just for me, he sent me to bed. He didn't feel right going to a bedroom on second floor where I was sleeping, but, of course, he wasn't going to leave me here and go over to the main house. He slept on the couch. I made a bed for him, but I'm afraid it wasn't too comfortable for someone who had to get up early and put in a full day's work. I fixed a big breakfast for him this morning, and he said he would come in for lunch when I told him he needed a warm meal. Oh, Grandma, it's so much fun acting like a wife." Giggling, she felt her grandma would understand so she continued, "I went to the main house this morning and remade his bed, where he had been sleeping. It wasn't bad, but I just wanted to put my touches on it. Am I being terribly silly?"

"Oh, Sweetie, you sound so much like me when I came to the ranch as a newlywed. I wanted to do everything for Noah and to touch everything he had touched. Of course, I was a college graduate, which is quite different from a seventeen-year-old. You act so much more mature than I did when I became a wife and a nurse to Jeremiah. Just be careful you don't miss out on a wonderful part of growing up, Liz, like a lot of those rare high school experiences that are remembered the rest of your life.

But listen, Dear, we should be home between 5:30 and 6:00 o'clock. Maybe we'll stop and get something to eat in town before coming on to the ranch."

"No, Grandma, please don't do that. I want to fix dinner for all of you so I can show off my cooking skills. Will you please come on home and let me do that? I promise I won't poison any of you," she giggled.

"If you want to do that, we'll certainly come on home. I'm sure everyone will feel more comfortable there. We'll see you this evening then, Sweetie. We all love you."

"I love you, too. Bye, Grandma."

Liz had found some beef barbeque in the refrigerator, so for lunch she planned to fix Josh a hot sandwich, a bowl of soup, and a quartered apple. It was ready and waiting when he came in a little past noon, quickly apologized for being late, and dropped into his chair at the table. He let out a big sigh.

"Has there been some trouble this morning?" she asked, "You look exhausted."

"A couple of the horses found a break in the fence of the paddock and decided to take a stroll around the meadow with the cattle. It took three of us to finally corral them and get the fence mended. They had to be the feistiest ones of the whole lot." Laughing, he told her about trying to approach the runaways, and just when the guys would get to within about six feet, the horses would just whinny at them as they took off at a gallop. "It was getting a little frustrating by the time we were finally successful with the lasso and brought them in, so we put them in their stalls while we fixed the fence."

Liz told him about her grandma's call and that they were all planning to be home for dinner tonight. "I'll most likely be busy most of the afternoon fixing a good meal for a very tired bunch, including you, of course." She gave him a big smile and a hug. "You'll always be my knight in shining armor even if you can't catch a feisty horse who just wants to take a stroll in the meadow and smell the wildflowers," she laughed as she patted his cheek.

Josh quickly turned his chair away from the table and pulled her onto his lap. "Liz Becker, you are really asking for it. I just wish I could think of something to do that would be appropriate. This will have to do, though," he chuckled as he turned her into a position where he could give her a kiss but only landed one on her cheek. "That's all you deserve after your unflattering remarks."

"If you want to eat tonight with the family, you'd better be good to me. How much do you have to do this afternoon? Could you come in and take a nap before they get here? You wouldn't want them to think that you can't handle the ranch...or me." Giggling, she tried to jump off his lap, but he had her anchored with his arms around her waist. "Josh, you'd better let me go right now!"

"You're a little feisty yourself, Miss Becker. Maybe I should bring the lasso in and see how you'd feel with a rope around your neck." Feeling her body tense rather suddenly, he turned so he could see her face while still holding her on his lap. "I was just kidding, Liz. You do know me well enough to realize that would never happen, don't you?" Grinning, he pulled her to him so her side was against his chest. He ran his fingers through her hair and then tilted her chin and kissed her gently on the lips this time. "Should this be permitted with no one around to chaperone us? I could get carried away if this went on for very long,"

She tried to get up, but he kept her in a tight hold as he kissed her cheek, her forehead and that tender spot below the ear. She shivered as he nibbled her earlobe. "Josh, you'd best get back to work before you do scare me. You wouldn't really try something, would you?"

Releasing her, he chuckled as he stood up, put on his hat and jacket and headed for the door. "I'm sorry if I scared you, Liz, but I'd never take advantage of you or any situation where my family has put their trust in me. I may have gone a little too far with my teasing again, but I wish you knew how much I respect you, adore you, and that I would do anything in my power to protect you. You certainly are a temptation, though," he chuckled. As he went out the door, he looked back at her and grinned. "Bye, Feisty."

Liz stood pondering Josh's actions for a few minutes, but realized that he was just up to his teasing again. She had too much work to do this afternoon to worry about what didn't happen. It did concern her a little, though, and she wondered what she would've done if he'd been serious. *I'm going to be more careful around him from now on because I can't expect him to do all the backing away. After all, he is a man and I have to be responsible for my actions, too. I don't want another Sergio confrontation, but maybe I started it just now when I gave him the hug. I don't want to miss all those hugs and kisses, but I can be a little more selective about when and where I get a little feisty.* She was laughing about that as she went to clear the lunch dishes and then start her plans for dinner.

Josh had been able to finish the chores early, and he came in around 5:45 all freshly showered and dressed in clean clothes. She had almost everything ready, the table was set, and she'd found some irises blooming which made a pretty centerpiece.

"Can I help with anything, Liz?" he asked. "I just noticed Noah's car about ready to pull into the driveway, and I think I saw Jon's coming right behind it."

She looked at him in surprise when she realized he had used her real name at least once at noon and again just now instead of one of his pet names for her. "Is everything all right, Josh, or did I do something wrong again?"

"Everything is fine, Sweetheart. Just thought I'd see if I could get a rise out of you since you didn't seem to notice when I called you Liz once or twice during lunch. I'd show you how fine, but the family is almost at the door so I'll behave myself. You had better do the same." He chuckled as he filled a pitcher with ice and water and headed to the table to fill the glasses. She hadn't asked, but he saw that it needed to be done, and that was one thing he could do right in a kitchen.

The family was really tired and hungry, and they were delighted with the deep dish of baked chicken that Liz had fixed along with scalloped potatoes, broccoli, and a fresh salad. Everybody was *really* congratulating her for a job well done when she brought her special dessert to the table which was a cherry cobbler with ice cream.

There had been no lag in the conversation with news from the hospital and then the tale of the runaway horses which brought a big chuckle from Noah. "Those two seem to be ready to cause trouble whenever Brent and Joseph aren't around, and this isn't the first time they've found a way to get out of the paddock. It's a quick way to learn, however, which ones to keep your eye on. I should've warned you, but it slipped my mind when I was giving you the normal routine to follow, and it has always surprised me how they can find a spot to escape through only when Brent and Joseph aren't around.

"I'll remember to watch them, Noah, and I surely appreciate the opportunity to learn so much about the ranch and its operation."

Christy wanted to help clean up the dishes but everyone insisted that she go sit down or that Jon get her home to bed. They'd gone by the office to pick up Jon's car on the way from the hospital, so those two headed home soon after eating and getting some more clean clothes for Marge and Brent from the main house. Eleanor had taken one change last night, but they'd need more if Marge remained insistent that she wouldn't go home without Joseph. A motel room, not too far from the hospital, had been reserved so they could shower and get a good comfortable nap now and then, so clean clothes would also feel good.

Smiling, Josh insisted that he still had some energy left so he would help Liz clean up her mess in the kitchen. "I didn't make that big of a mess, you, you big meany!" She had a cloth napkin in her hand this time and started chasing him as she had the night before.

"Here we go again," he laughed as he picked up a couple of dishes from the table and headed for the sink area. Noah and Eleanor enjoyed the antics for a few minutes, but soon dismissed themselves to go relax in front of the TV.

When Josh and Liz finished their fun together and had the kitchen all cleaned up, they found the two asleep in their chairs. They patted their shoulders to wake them and send them off to bed. Josh had wanted to spend a little time with Liz, but his eyes wouldn't stay open either. He smiled sheepishly, kissed her cheek, and headed for the main house.

"*He probably doesn't know it, but he's going to have a nice big breakfast waiting for him in the morning again,* Liz was contemplating as she climbed the stairs to her bedroom. She set the alarm on buzzing, not ringing, so she wouldn't wake her grandparents when she got up and went to the kitchen. As she said her prayers for Joseph and the family, she also thanked God for giving her this opportunity. *This is exactly what I want my future to be, no matter what anyone says, Dear Jesus, and I certainly hope it's in your plans for me.*

Chapter Twenty-Three

When Liz's alarm clock started buzzing the next morning, she smiled as she realized she'd been dreaming of being Josh's wife and sleeping in his arms. She was immediately out of bed and pulling on her jeans and sweat shirt. She tried to be very quiet as she went down the stairs to the kitchen where she would get the key to the main house.

Just as she reached for it, however, she heard a very familiar voice, "And just what do you think you're doing, Young Lady?" Her grandmother had quietly come into the room and Liz turned to face her. She saw that she was smiling, but Liz was pretty sure that her trip to the main house was not going to happen.

"I was planning to fix Josh a good breakfast again

this morning, Grandma, before he goes to do the chores."

"Well, Sweetie, that is not necessary because Josh will be coming here fairly soon for his breakfast just like he has since he arrived Wednesday. You can help feed him by setting the table, getting the butter out of the refrigerator and the syrup from the pantry. You may do the honors, also, of pouring the orange juice. We're fixing pancakes this morning, along with bacon and eggs, so you can help me get it all ready.

I'm sorry if I'm spoiling your fun, Liz, but I think you'd better slow down this project of yours wanting to treat Josh as if he were your husband. I don't think Josh is ready for that, and you certainly aren't with two years of school left after this one, so let's just try to cool those hormones a bit so you can be the age you're supposed to be.

And, another thing for you to consider is that Josh has his hands pretty full right now handling all the responsibilities of this ranch. He is fresh out of college with no one around to guide him except Grandpa. I understand from Noah that he is doing a very good job, but it hasn't even been four full days yet, so I don't think you should put any more weight on his shoulders by pursuing your dream of the future, whatever that may be."

"I'm sorry, Grandma. You're right, of course, but

I had been so depressed when I got here. When Josh told me that he and Melanie had broken up because she didn't want to get married for at least two or three years, I couldn't believe my ears. Then he said that if he had to wait two years for a wife, he was going to wait for me, and I was completely shocked that God had brought us back together. I guess I really got carried away. I'll get the table set."

When Josh showed up at the door a few minutes later, Liz gave him a nice friendly smile, and then quietly served him his breakfast as if she were a server in a restaurant. "You're awfully prim and proper this morning, Miss Becker. Did you sleep on the wrong side of your bed or get up on the wrong side of it, whatever the saying is?"

Liz looked at her grandmother, almost begging for help, so Eleanor in her very loving but straightforward way, said, "Liz and I had a little talk this morning, Josh. I informed her that you had your hands pretty full handling all the details of the ranch so I felt she shouldn't add anymore concerns on your shoulders right now. I'm just afraid that my sensitive little granddaughter doesn't quite know where the middle of the road is."

Josh couldn't keep from laughing as he said, "Come here a minute, Liz, I want to tell you something." As she approached him, he took her hand and pulled her down on his lap. He could tell she was embarrassed because her grandmother was in the room, but he wanted to make just one thing clear to her. "Princess, you could never be a burden on my shoulders, but I do have a lot on my mind right now, as your grandmother said, and I don't want to make any mistakes caring for the ranch. I'm so glad you came to me when you were troubled, and I think we're both happier now feeling that God wants us back together after the rather sad and upsetting experiences we each have had. So, for now, would you be my very sweet, mysterious Princess, and get me another cup of coffee, please." He set her on her feet and gave her a little push to send her on her way.

When he'd finished eating, he started toward the door. "Thank you, Dear Ladies, for another marvelous meal. I'm beginning to see why Jon is putting on weight with all the great cooks around here. I'm on my way now to see if I can work some of it off. I'll try my best to finish in time to attend church services. Adios."

"He's a wonderful young man, Liz, so much like his older brother in some ways, but entirely different in others. One is, and the other could be, a great addition to our family one day," she grinned, "but right now I see we have another hungry gentleman to feed a big ranch breakfast. Good morning, Noah."

"Good morning, Eleanor, My Dear." He gave

her a quick kiss on the cheek and then turned to look at Liz. "How is our youngest granddaughter this beautiful Sunday morning? Did I hear Josh say something about God wanting the two of you back together after rather sad upsetting experiences you both have had? Is there something you can discuss with us, or is it just between you and Josh?"

"Well, I was pretty upset when I arrived in Paris. Although I knew Mom and Dad were concerned about me, I couldn't talk to them. Then we were notified of Uncle Joseph being in the hospital and, of course, headed home. When I heard that Josh was here at the ranch, I just felt I had to talk to him alone. He's been so good at helping me understand the pains of growing up, and he was the only one I felt I could talk to. It's hard to talk about, Grandpa, but I had to confront and say goodbye to Sergio while we were in Barcelona. He turned out to be a completely different person than I thought he was when ..he ...ah...he...ah asked for something I couldn't or wouldn't give. I was so shocked and disappointed that I threw some of my drink in his face as I left the restaurant and returned to my room.

I've learned now that Josh had been told Tuesday night by this Melanie, whom he'd been dating, that she'd only considered them very good friends and she had no intentions of getting married for two, three, or maybe more years. Apparently, she wants to teach and be able to travel and just do her own thing. I don't know if it was just a coincidence, or God's plan, but the next morning he got the call from Jon about our need here. And then another miracle happened when Dad let me drive down to see him," she giggled. "We both feel that God brought us back together for a reason, but Josh also feels that God may still have other trials or experiences for us to face, but I'm quite sure now that my future is eventually going to be with him. I don't know why we both had to go through the unsatisfactory relationships, but maybe it was to show us exactly what we'd found in each other."

"Wow, that's quite a story, Sweetheart. I'm sorry, though, that you had to face that situation when you were so far from home. I wasn't sure, when I saw the two of you here together Friday night, what the ending of this little love affair was going to be, but I can see now that God's hand surely is in it, and I think the future looks rather bright. Things do seem to work out when we put our trust in God."

⤚

Noah and Eleanor had decided that they would follow Liz on her drive home later Sunday afternoon because they wanted to visit the hospital again. Marge had called them, before they'd left for church, to tell them that Joseph had made it through the night and

Dr. Wilder seemed very pleased with his progress. He's still in guarded condition but had been awake earlier and had talked to both her and Brent, and Christy had also been in with him after she and Jon had arrived. This made Noah and Eleanor even more anxious to see their son. They would most likely stay Sunday night and drive back Monday after they'd seen the doctor. Noah and Jon both have important clients coming in Tuesday morning so they'll need to come back for those appointments.

Josh had finished the morning chores and gotten to church just as the pastor prepared to make the opening remarks. He included Joseph's condition and asked for all their prayers on his behalf. Josh slipped in beside Liz and then gave her a big grin. "Did you get any more instructions from your grandmother after I left?" he whispered.

"No, but Grandfather had overheard a few of your remarks and coaxed some more of the information from me," she whispered back. They then became quiet to listen and learn, but Josh reached over and put her hand in his to hold during the sermon. He'd smiled and winked, which made her feel so loved and protected, but she was also dreading the necessity to return home later this afternoon and return to school tomorrow to possibly face Sergio.

∽

Josh came to ask if Liz would like to go riding, after he'd finished the rest of the work early Sunday afternoon. They rode out to the big stone that Christy had shown them last Thanksgiving, and they stopped there to talk for awhile. Josh could tell Liz was upset about having to go back home, so they discussed how she could handle the Sergio situation if and when something happened. He'd also tried to cheer her up with little jokes and stories, but then finally decided to tell her about his graduation coming up on June 3rd and that he was hoping he could get her father's permission so she can attend. She could share a room with his sister, Janice, and there would be plenty of chaperones. Since graduation would be on a Saturday morning, they would have to drive over there on Friday.

She was elated because it would give her something to look forward to. She told him that she was still talking to her folks about finishing school here in Hayes, but Josh tried to convince her that she should be with her parents. She gave him a very obstinate look which told him to mind his own business if he wasn't going to agree with her. He couldn't hold his chuckle, and she slapped his arm pretty hard, but then quickly apologized by kissing him.

When they reached the barn, Noah was waiting for them. Helping to get the horses in their stalls, he informed them that it was time for Liz to start toward home. Josh was almost afraid to look at Liz because he thought she would start crying. He was in for a big surprise when she came to him, gave him a big hug, told him she would see him when school was out, if not sooner, and headed for the house. Noah talked to Josh for a few minutes longer, since he would be there by himself for the night, and informed him that Eleanor had put his supper in the refrigerator at the main house. He could warm it in the microwave. He then walked to his car where Eleanor was waiting. Josh watched as Liz carried her bag to her car, turned to wave to him, and then the two cars pulled away. He had never felt so alone, but also content. because he had his princess back.

⤚

When Liz had gotten close to Colorado Springs, she'd called home on her cell phone, and Mary had told her that their parents were still at the hospital. Liz told her that she was going to go there, too, because she wanted to visit the chapel, and she would come home when their mom and dad did.

The news of Joseph's steady progress was wonderful to hear, but he still had a ways to go before he'd be completely out of danger. Liz went over to Christy to ask if she would like to go to the chapel, and Christy immediately agreed. She asked Jon if he wanted to come along.

"I'd love to but I think Brent needs to get away for awhile, too, so let's see if he'll go with us. Maybe we can go to the cafe for a drink or take a walk outside before or after we spend some time in the chapel. It's really a beautiful evening. Just give me a minute and I'll try to persuade him to go."

Brent hesitated a moment and then nodded toward his mother. "I'll just let her know where we're going and be right with you." They decided to go for a walk outside first before it got too late. There was a courtyard with a pool and large fountain, and it was delightful to listen to the water fall from the pineapple shaped top. They walked the paths which circle the area and saw that the perennials were beginning to sprout and the shrubs and trees were also budding out.

"This is the time of year when I love to ride the trails and view the mountains, the ponds, and the meadows because everything is saying that Spring is near and everything will soon be in full bloom. It gives hope that things will be fresh and new again for another great season," Christy remarked.

They then entered the chapel and found it so peaceful. They were silent as they all raised their prayers to God in their own way, and then they went to the cafeteria to get a few things to munch on, and a cool drink. They all felt refreshed when they returned to the family waiting room.

Dr. Wilder had been there while they'd been gone and the news was continuing to be very good. He'd told the family that Joseph had had a very close call, but it appeared that by morning he'd be out of danger and could look forward to going home in a week or so. If the family would agree, however, he'd like for Joseph to stay in the hospital for a few extra days until he was definitely strong enough to have the carotid artery surgery. If not, they could schedule it later, but he warned that they shouldn't wait too long.

Marge and Noah wanted Joseph to help them make the decision, so the two of them went in to see him together. The three decided that as long as he was in the hospital, he might as well stay and get it all done. He could then go home knowing the entire ordeal was over and he could concentrate on the rehab therapy he would be facing.

∽

Brent told Jon he needed to talk to him so they went to another waiting room that was empty. "Jon, I'm at a loss as to what to do. I'm going to need another full time person I can rely on to run the ranch with me, because Dad is *not* going back to doing the work like he has for all these years. I'm going to see that he and Mom take the trips that they've wanted to go on for quite a while now, and really try to enjoy themselves before it's too late. I guess what I'm trying to say or ask is, do you think Josh would consider giving up his dream of helping run your family farm and come help me run the ranch? Noah has really been impressed with him the last few days, and I'd love to have him as my partner so I can enjoy that wonderful sense of humor as well as his knowledge of ranch duties," he chuckled. "Do you happen to know how determined he is to work with your dad?"

"Wow, Brent, I don't know what to say. I do know that Josh loves the ranch and was so moved when he was asked to come and help out. All I can do is ask him, and also check with Dad to see what his feelings are about the future of the farm. He has been very pleased with Matt and the work that he's been doing, and he also said that Janice has been helping out quite a bit, so it may not be a huge inconvenience to lose Josh, but we'll just have to check it out with both of them."

"Would you be willing to do that, or do you want me to approach Josh?" Brent asked.

"Why don't you let me talk to him tomorrow and get his take on the whole idea? If he would like to stay at the ranch, we can then talk to Dad. I'll try to get an answer for you right away so you'll know if you have to make other arrangements. Right now, though, I think I'd better find out what your sister's plans are for tonight, because I have to be at the office rather early in the morning as well as Tuesday. Would you like to drive home, Brent, and see for yourself that things are under control? Christy can stay with your mom if you would like to do that."

"No, I trust Josh to take care of things and I just can't leave here even though they say Dad appears out of danger. Mom was so scared that first night, when Dad hadn't come to by the exact time the doctor had predicted, and she really thought she was going to lose him. I have to be here for her. You go ahead and take Christy home so she can get a good night's rest again. Mom and I both got some rest last night and we'll sleep better tonight, I'm sure. I just want to thank you, Jon, for all you've done already and are still going to do."

❧

After Jon had finished with his two clients the next day, he drove out to the ranch to see Josh. They sat on the deck, enjoying the beautiful spring day, and Jon told him about Brent's dilemma. "Would you even want to consider coming here and giving up your dream of running our farm some day?"

"Oh, Jon, can you even imagine what an opportunity that would be for me--to be able to help run this ranch? I fell in love with this place the first time I saw it, but in my wildest dreams I could never have thought I'd have the chance to work as a hired hand, let alone help manage it. Dad is still young and in good health, so do you think he could manage with Matt there, along with Janice and the extra help he hires? Jacob can get out there and help, too. I think he owes that to our folks."

"Well, it sounds like we'd better get Dad on the phone and find out how he feels about all this. I can see that this would also help solve your problem with Liz during the next two years if the long distance dating is going to be happening. Right?"

Josh had told Jon about Melanie wanting to teach for at least two or three years with no wedding plans, plus his seeing Liz again and her confiding in him about Sergio. "It just seems like God wanted us to see what was out there and then let us decide if the two years were too long to wait. Since she came running into my arms Friday afternoon, I have made up my mind that the little princess is going to be mine in 2008."

"Have you talked to Liz about this?"

"A little, but she doesn't need much encouragement," he said, laughing. "She tried so discreetly to be my doting wife when her dad let her drive down here last Friday. It was cute, and she is actually very good at cooking, making beds, hugging, and even a kiss or two. She is going to make a wonderful wife someday and I'm planning on her being mine. If I'm going to be here at the ranch, I'll talk to Dr. Becker, the first chance I get, and see how he'd feel if we dated for the next two years. If he doesn't really like the idea, the way I feel right now, I will still be around when she graduates, and then I'll claim the princess as my wife."

Just then one of the men called from the barn, "Josh, could you come down here. I'm afraid we have a little problem."

"Duty calls. Can you stick around for a few minutes until I find out what is bothering them this time?"

"Sure. I'll hang around for a little while."

Chapter Twenty-Four

While he waited, Jon got his father on the phone and discussed his conversation with Brent. He told him of Brent's concern about the ranch and how he would need an Assistant Manager because of Joseph's health.

Tom quickly realized where this could be leading. He'd known how impressed Josh had been with the ranch, and now, after working there for only a few days, a position is open that would allow him to be there day after day. He can only wonder if this is another miracle God is giving to Josh to give his future real meaning. "Jon," he asked, "what really are your true feelings on this? Do you think Josh would be more interested in helping Brent manage the ranch than our family farm?"

"Josh is, as you would guess, Dad, torn between his obligation to you and his love of the ranch. Noah has been very impressed with his handling of the ranch this past week, and Brent seems to feel he would be a great partner. Not only that," he chuckled, "but it appears that the love affair between Josh and Liz is back on, so if Josh is here at the ranch, the long distance affair wouldn't be quite so traumatic.

In fact, I understand that Liz had been trying to convince her parents to let her finish high school in Hayes long before Josh was ever in the picture. It's going to be a long two years for those two, but Josh seems to have his head on straight now, and Liz is so mature for her age. Josh is definitely serious, right now at least, about her becoming his wife in 2008, whether David will give his permission for them to date or not. He says he'll still be around when Liz graduates, and then she'll be his wife.

So, Dad, it comes down to how you feel about all this, and what the situation is at the farm. I know that Josh would stay with the original plan if he thought you'd be without any future help and really wanted him to work with you. Do you still feel that Matt is a good prospect for the manager position there, especially if he and Janice were to get together?"

Tom had listened quietly and hesitated only slightly before he spoke. "I could tell that Joshua had fallen in love with the ranch the first time we were there, and your mother and I have talked about the possibility of him wanting something other than this farm. With Liz in the picture again," he laughed, "that only adds fuel to the fire, doesn't it? Oh my, but what an uncertain path we trod as we try to follow God's plan for our lives.

But God works in mysterious ways, Jon, and this opportunity opening up at the exact time Joshua is able to take it just has to be one of God's miracles at work. I can't think of any way I could justify my refusing him this opportunity of a lifetime. Did he ask you to talk to me on his behalf because he was afraid he would hurt my feelings?"

"No, Dad, he didn't. We were both going to talk to you, but one of the hired hands had a problem and Josh had to go to the barn. I took the opportunity to call and let you in on what was going on so you wouldn't have to make a rather quick decision. If you want to talk to Mom about the situation, I'll have Josh call you back later today or he could wait until tomorrow."

"That would probably be best that I inform Frances, but I know what our decision will be. One has to accept the opportunities he wants when they're offered or he'll regret it the rest of his life. We'll miss both of you, but we're so lucky that you aren't so far away that we can't get together over a weekend. Seriously,

Jon, I think being close to you will be just what Joshua needs. You've been a wonderful big brother to him, and I'm so glad that you'll continue to be there for him. The big change in his life recently, after witnessing what he realizes was a miracle, seems to be a lasting one, and Liz has been another great influence.

As far as Matthew is concerned, I've really become quite attached to that boy, as has Janice," he chuckled, "and it appears that they might be just as determined as Joshua to get married in a year or two. Janice has also been talking about taking correspondence courses with Matthew and has given up her dream of being a vet. She seems to love working with us, or maybe it's just Matthew, but she has learned very quickly. With some help from Jacob and the hired hands, we'll be fine.

So Josh stayed at the ranch. Joseph came home from the hospital and has been doing well. He and Marge are already planning a short trip when he gets released by the doctor and he has finished the first required follow-up therapy. Brent and Josh have worked extremely well together and now Memorial Day has arrived.

Josh can hardly wait for Liz to get there. He had talked to Dr. Becker on the phone and got his permission for Liz to go to his graduation, but he has something else he wants to talk to him about this weekend. He and Brent were busy when they arrived so he didn't see Liz until dinner time. He put his arm across her shoulders and led her to the chair next to his. She smiled, but he could see the blush coming on. He dropped his arm from her shoulders and just held the chair for her.

He realized that before he could talk to Liz about their future, he first had to talk to Dr. Becker. After they'd eaten, Josh approached Liz's dad, shaking in his boots, of course, and asked, "Dr. Becker, could I talk to you for a few minutes, please?"

"Certainly, Josh," he answered quickly and led the way to the library. After closing the door, he turned to face this obviously nervous young man. "I hope this isn't bad news, Josh, but what is it that has you a little more nervous than usual?" He had, of course, noticed Josh and Liz together and had seen her face turning a pretty shade of red. Had she just been embarrassed by his show of affection or could there be something else going on? He is very anxious to hear what Josh has to say.

"I hope you won't consider it bad news, Sir, but I'll come right to the point. I'd like to ask if you would give your permission for Liz and me to have a long engagement. I'd love to give her an engagement ring and then maybe we could plan to get married July 5, 2008. If you happen to remember, July 5th was the day I woke up, after the concussion, and saw Liz sitting beside my bed. She became my mysterious princess that day because she wouldn't tell if she'd given me a kiss to wake me up. She still hasn't told me, so I've continued to call her my mysterious princess."

"I wondered how you'd come up with that pet name, and I even caught myself using it in one of my conversations with her," he chuckled. "It really sort of fits her. So, you think my then sixteen-year-old daughter gave you a magic kiss and that did the trick, huh? That's pretty interesting. I guess it's a good thing she's seventeen now or she might be in trouble for violating our rules." He couldn't stop a chuckle.

"She told me about that rule, but much later. Dr. Wilder, however, made a remark about a fairy princess, but after he glanced at Liz I noticed he quickly got down to serious doctoring. He may have the answer, but I think I'll wait and let her tell me. Do you know that saying about a girl chasing a guy until he catches her? Well, I'm not sure who has been doing the chasing, but I want to catch her and never let her go."

Dr. Becker couldn't keep from laughing, mostly from relief. "Whew, you had me a little worried there, Josh, but I do know that little saying and I'd say it's been a little of both. I can't deny that Rachel and I have been concerned about the age difference and, of course, the possibility that you might want more than Liz should be ready to give. It appears that it was

Sergio who wanted more than she would give, however. I guess we've always been a little over-protective of Liz because we almost lost her the year she turned six."

"I hadn't heard about that, Dr. Becker. Would you please tell me about it? I want to learn as much as I can about her."

"Well, Mary was in school and seemed to bring all the childhood diseases home and pass them on to Liz. We thought that was all right because she'd be immune then when she started to school the following year. We'd had unusual fall weather that year, but when she came down with this very high fever, we initially thought it was another normal disease, but that hadn't been the case. We soon realized it was something that I couldn't diagnose and we called in a specialist in childhood diseases. After several days of this high fever, in and out of comas, and definitely puzzling to all us doctors, it was finally determined from one of the later blood samples that she had a very rare case of pneumonia.

She was a very sick girl for almost a month, and then it took her another several months to get her strength back. That's why we held her out of school for another year. She was really upset with us because she'd wanted to go to school like her big brother and sister. But, even at that age, she begged to come down to the ranch and spend her time in the wide open spaces, as she called them. She spent a lot of time with Eleanor and loved to be in the kitchen with her and to follow her wherever she went. She would only go riding or be with the other kids if Eleanor was there with her, and that lasted for several years whenever we were here at the ranch. At home, she had her nose in a book most of the time."

"Wow, I had no idea she'd been through such a horrible experience. Not that being with Eleanor was horrible, but the illness must've been quite traumatic for such a little girl. I can certainly understand her closeness to Eleanor a little better now, but do you think being committed to a long-term engagement would be too much for her since she'll have her school work and other obligations, too?"

"She's fine, strong and healthy now, Josh, and from all that she's told us, you've been nothing but attentive and protective toward her, even with a few teaching conversations, we understand," he chuckled. "We realize that you are her knight in shining armor, but two years seems like quite a while for a long distance romance to truly survive, especially at her age. Do you really think the two of you can handle that?"

"She definitely feels that God has brought us back together for a reason. Your family comes here occasionally, I could drive up to see her on my weekends off, and now that Liz has a car, maybe you would let her drive down here once in a while. I know she'd like to finish her schooling here in Hayes, but I've told her I thought she needed to be with her mom during these teen years. She more or less told me to butt out, if I didn't agree with her, but I got my two cents in anyway," he chuckled.

"Thanks, Josh, that's very thoughtful of you, but Rachel and I have been considering her almost constant request to come here and finish high school. She hasn't been happy in the schools up home for at least the last two years, except for her language classes. It has really been a struggle for her since this Sergio affair. Noah and Eleanor would be thrilled to have her live with them, and there wouldn't be a better teacher and guardian than Eleanor for a girl who doesn't want to go to college. To quote her words, 'I just want to get married and be a good wife and mother.' Of course, I assume you knew that," he chuckled. "Eleanor told us she hoped she hadn't stepped over the line, but that she'd had a talk with Liz about her act of being your wife the weekend she drove down to talk to you about her problem with Sergio and Joseph was in the hospital. When you asked to talk to me tonight, my first thought was maybe we'd been a little too trusting when we'd left the two of you un-chaperoned, but her actions and temperament at home hadn't given any hint of anything being wrong."

Josh was grinning when he said, "Dr. Becker, you don't need to worry about me ever taking advantage of Liz, but it was so cute watching her acting out her role of being my wife. I think she really believed she was being discreet, but I understood what she was doing and really appreciated the love she put into caring for me. I'm not saying that it'll be easy to keep from wanting her, but I do think if we could see each other more often, it might be a little easier than trying to make up for lost time if we just see each other now and then. Besides, we both know your daughter has a very strong moral character, after hearing how she very efficiently handled that punk Sergio when he tried to take advantage of the situation. I don't want to be the recipient of her rage." he chuckled.

"I thought I had seen a moral character in you, Josh, but I had been so wrong about Sergio. That was really a shock when you called and explained what had happened in Spain. But, now to answer your question, I guess I see no harm in trying a long-term engagement, if that is what Liz wants. From all the conversations she has had with her mother and me, we know she feels that God has led you back to each other, but I don't want to see her pressured into this long-term thing just for *your* satisfaction."

"No Sir. I'll be very careful to let her decide if this is what she really wants."

"Wow, I may just have to retire from the hospital in Colorado Springs, move down to Hayes, and open an office to take care of my grandchildren, plus great nieces and nephews. I've heard that Brent gave Susan a ring on her birthday the other night, and they're planning a wedding later this year, or early next year." Smiling, he continued, "Brad has always loved the ranch and says he wants to either be here or at the Law Office, so why should Rachel and I stay up there in Colorado Springs? We never know where Mary will settle, if she follows her dream to become a doctor, but she could even join me in a practice here in Hayes, too."

Putting his arm around Josh's shoulders, as they left the library, David said, "I guess this is a welcome of another Holcomb into the Hayes family, and we're very happy to include you, Josh." Chuckling, he said, "One thing this requires, however, is that you start calling me by my first name, until it becomes Dad, of course. No more Dr. Becker or Sir. I'll let Noah and Joseph inform you as to how you should address them."

"Thank you so much, Sir--ah--David. It'll probably take me a while to get used to it, but I guess it shouldn't start until I get the ring on her finger anyway."

"You don't really expect that to be a problem, do you?" he laughed.

Chapter Twenty-Five

The following weekend was Josh's graduation so Liz planned to stay with Noah and Eleanor so she wouldn't have to make another trip from Colorado Springs. Every afternoon, after playing tennis, going for a ride or a swim, just the two of them would sit on the deck to enjoy a cool drink. It seemed more and more like they were really supposed to be together.

After Josh had been notified that he needed to drive to the college on Thursday to get his robe and go through the short rehearsal Friday morning, Liz planned to ride with Jon and Christy on Friday. Josh's parents, siblings, and four grandparents would be coming, too. All of the reservations had been made at the beautifully restored hotel near campus for the twelve of them to have rooms and dinner on Friday night. Janice and Liz were sharing a room, Josh and Jacob were sharing another, and the four couples were truly enjoying seeing the historic renovations that had been made in their rooms and throughout the hotel.

The graduation ceremony began at 10:30 Saturday morning with the band playing some patriotic songs and then ending with the school song. Of course, everyone stood, sang, and cheered. Several professors spoke about their classes and the outstanding students they'd had the privilege of instructing.

The valedictorian was quite a surprise to Josh when he saw that Melanie Grant was being introduced. He really hoped it didn't register with Liz, because he hadn't mentioned her last name, but could there possibly be more than one Melanie in a graduating class? *Oh well, Liz knows that romance is over, if there ever was one, and she is the one I'm committed to now and forever.* He didn't hear much of what Melanie said, but it apparently had been quite good because she got several rounds of applause during and after her presentation. It was just another sign that she would be a great teacher, and he wished her the best.

And then his name was called, and the person sitting next to him had to give him a punch in the arm and inform him he was being called to the stage. "What in the world is this about?" he said softly as he made his way up the aisle.

"Every year, the college professors select a student who they feel has given of himself or herself beyond the normal," his Agriculture professor began. "We feel that Josh has truly done this over the four years he has been with us. He started helping a new football coach by practicing with the players and teaching them plays they were unfamiliar with. Josh knew those plays because our new football coach had been his high school coach. He did this for three years, and only because of a riding accident, he decided not to be involved this year. After all, why would he want to expose himself to another season of facing those big, rough and tough football guys?"

There was a roar from the crowd and everyone cheered. The football team was well represented at this graduation ceremony.

"Josh also gave of his time to help other students in his classes who would, now and then, have a problem with a certain phase of the study. I know it happened in the class I was teaching. And, during this last semester, he has also worked with the pastor of our chapel by visiting with students who had been brought to the pastor's attention by a friend, a family member, or a teacher. Without even knowing it, he caused one girl to completely change her life and dedicate it to God and a mission in nursing." There was another round of applause.

"He conscientiously joined a group of our students over Spring Break who was going to the Gulf Coast to help with the clean-up after the hurricane last Fall. I understand that it was long hours and hard, dirty work, but I never heard one word of a complaint from Josh, although I did from a few others," he chuckled.

"And then, in April, he relinquished the rest of his carefree college days to help out again. I say 'carefree' because he'd had sufficient credits to graduate in January, but he had chosen to finish the year to see how much more he could learn and to continue working with the pastor. This time he was called upon to help his sister-in-law's family through a health crisis. By managing their ranch, the son and the rest of the family could be at the hospital where their loved one was facing open heart by-pass surgery. Josh had been studying all the techniques for running his family's farm one day, so he was the perfect candidate to fill this position. I understand that he has been asked to be the Assistant Manager of the ranch and has accepted. The heart patient can now relax and concentrate on getting stronger and soon enjoy life by traveling with his wife whenever they like, because the ranch will be in good hands with Josh working beside their son. Josh, we're thrilled to be able to tell your story and to present you with this plaque in appreciation of all you have done for those who have benefited from your help over the last four years. We wish you the very best, wherever the future may lead."

Josh was speechless and could only whisper a "Thank You so very much," but he got a standing ovation along with a lot of cheers from the football section.

After the diplomas were presented, Josh joined the family for lunch in the banquet room of the college. He was still in shock and so quiet that no one could believe that this was their Josh, the rebel and clown of the family. They all realized, however, that he had changed in many ways this past year. It had all started when he'd met Liz last July and then culminated at the accident scene when he'd experienced the miracle of the unharmed baby. He had then accepted Jesus into his life. They were all so proud of their new graduate.

Many of the graduates and their families were milling around after lunch trying to see their classmates for possibly the last time. Josh happened to catch sight of two or three of the big burley football players who had teased him continually about his infatuation with a little sixteen-year-old. He grabbed Liz's hand and told the others they'd see them later back at the farm. "I have a few friends that I want to meet Liz."

"Hey, Jake, I'd like you to meet the one who was my riding companion when I was thrown off the horse and taken to the hospital last July. This is Elizabeth Becker, the cutest and sweetest little seventeen-year-old in the world. Liz, this is one of the linemen on the football team that I had to teach a few things when we were both freshmen," he chuckled.

"Hi, Jake. I'm really glad to meet you. I'm also glad that you were on the same team as Josh and not coming at him from the other direction," she giggled.

"You actually found a beautiful, intelligent girl who knows a little about football, too? Aren't you the lucky one?" He turned and yelled across to a group of guys standing together a few yards away. "Hey, you big hunks of lard, come here and meet the little filly our Josh is in love with."

At least half-a-dozen guys started toward them, laughing and joking. When they had reached them, they were soon starting to ogle and admire, but it didn't take long for Josh to bring them down to correct behavior. "Listen closely, Guys, this is Elizabeth Becker, a young seventeen-year-old who is unfamiliar with your usual conversations and actions. She was my riding companion when I was thrown off the horse back in July. She is very precious to me, and I ask that you treat her with respect or please just leave quickly without another word out of your mouth. Understood?"

"Sure, Josh, we understand," one of the largest guys Liz had ever seen quietly spoke up. "We're really glad to meet the little fil--riding companion who was with you when you were thrown off the horse. We've missed him this year, Miss Becker, because he didn't want some more ribs hurt or another arm broken by us heavyweights."

"Yeah," another said, "and we want to congratulate you on the recognition you got up there today, Josh. You really deserved it. How is everything going at the ranch?"

"It's going really great, Guys. I'm not really sure I earned the plaque today, but it was quite an honor to be recognized. Now, I just wanted you to know that I wasn't lying about the cutest little sixteen-year-old, who is now seventeen, and still only has eyes for me," he chuckled. He looked at Liz and winked as he put his arm around her waist and gave her a little squeeze. He hoped she realized how much he admired her.

"Remember, we know where you can be found, Josh, and who knows when you may find us on your doorstep," another laughed as he started to walk away. "Keep track of us who are going to the NFL, and maybe you can come see us play if we ever get to Denver."

"We'll really try to do that, Kevin. If you have time to drop us a note or telephone us when you get your schedules, we'll try our best to get there. We wish all of you the best of luck in your future, whether it's in the NFL or something completely different."

The last one to leave approached slowly with his outstretched hand. "I've really felt honored getting to know you, Josh, and I do appreciate all you did for the team. I especially want to thank you for the personal help I received, perhaps indirectly, but help none the less. I just want to say Good Luck to both of you and may God bless. Maybe you haven't heard, but your great outreach work with Pastor Behrens, plus your personal example over the last four years, touched a few of us rowdy football players, too. Do you remember the night you dropped in the cafe and caught us drinking? Well, you might be interested to know that your wise words that night were the turning point for several of us."

"Now, that *does* warrant the plaque!" Josh laughed. "Thanks so much for sharing that with me, Chris, and I wish you continued happiness with Christ in your life."

'Well, I won't be going to the NFL. I really enjoyed getting to play while in college, but my family owns a business that I'll be joining now. I'm really looking forward to getting back home and helping out since that has always been my dream."

"I'm really happy for you, Chris, and maybe

we'll see you in the bleachers in Denver one of these days."

"I plan to follow the future of those in the NFL as closely as I can, so maybe we will get to Denver at the same time. I'll look forward to that."

"I will, too, Chris. I really enjoyed getting to know all of you and it's a little hard to say Goodbye, but with something to look forward to, it isn't quite so final."

Chapter Twenty-Six

It was a beautiful June afternoon to drive back to the farm. It would have been too long a trip to have gone all the way to Hayes, so Jon, Christy, Josh and Liz planned to spend the night at the farm and then drive on to Hayes on Sunday. Josh had been so thrilled to have Liz at his graduation, and they talked about the different events on the way home. To Josh's chagrin, Liz had noticed that Melanie Grant was the valedictorian and asked if she was truly the one he had dated.

"Yes, Princess, she was the Melanie I was involved with for those three months, but I realize now it was not love or anything close. I had no idea she would be the valedictorian."

"She gave a very good oration, and everyone seemed to be listening intently to what she was saying.

I'm glad you had a chance to know her and work with her. I think she'll be a very good teacher."

"I guess it was God's will that I got to know her because I would've never had the chance to work with the pastor and the students, like I did, if it hadn't been for her. That was an amazing experience that I won't soon forget. So many of the ones I talked to were the same as I had been, so sure they could do everything by themselves, some resented their parents for interfering in their lives, and some of them didn't want to talk to *me* either. I wish I could recall the different tactics I used to get their attention, but I think God put the words in my mouth so I was talking for Him. I was always thrilled if I saw them in church after I'd met with them, but I guess the most surprising was April, to whom the professor referred, or maybe it would be Chris today telling of the changes in the football team. That just about blew my mind. It was a rather disappointing sight that I walked in on that night in the cafe, so if I made a difference in only one of their lives, I'm thankful."

"That was exciting to hear Chris telling you about it, and I'm so proud of you, Josh. I know God is, too. I wish, or maybe I should say I hope that I can be a better disciple for Him this next year. Maybe when I change schools, it will give me a better opportunity to do that."

"Did you say a change in schools, Liz? When did this change in your plans happen?"

"Oh, Josh, I guess I've been so excited about going to your graduation that I forgot to tell you. Mom and Dad have agreed to let me come and stay with Grandma and Grandpa and finish high school in Hayes. Isn't that wonderful? I'll get to see you as often as you want to see me, and we can talk face to face instead of on the phone or e-mail. I am really looking forward to being at the ranch and learning more about Hayes and the family involvement in the town. Maybe we can do the research together."

"Wow, I don't know how you kept that a secret. You've been working on getting that done for quite some time. When do you think you'll move down?"

"I may bring my things down over the 4th of July. I'll have to get registered at school and see if there are any medical tests, shots, or exams I have to take before school starts. I'd think they would take my records from home, but Mom says there may be different rules in every county as to what they require, how they enroll and when you can select your classes."

"Well, Princess, I'm thrilled that I'll have you so close that we can go on dates and spend time together at the ranch, but I still feel that most young girls your age should be with their family, or especially their mother, during their teen years. I must admit, however, that you'll be in very competent hands with Eleanor and Noah," he chuckled.

"Oh, Josh, you are such a tease. I know I needed Grandma to set me straight when I came to see you over that weekend back in April, but I was so upset about Sergio and his bad-boy tactics that I went overboard when I realized God had brought us back together. I'm going to be a good student, a good granddaughter, and a very good friend to a rather ornery, but handsome, fellow whose graduation I just attended," she giggled.

"I'm going to hold you to that, Miss Becker, so nothing can get out of hand."

It was about 5:30 when they reached the farm. Jacob and Janice had left ahead of the rest so were the first ones to get there. Jon and Christy pulled in, with the Holcomb grand-parents, just ahead of Tom and Frances with the Shelley grandparents. Josh and Liz arrived about 45 minutes later since they had talked to several other classmates before starting home.

Matt surprised them by fixing burgers on the grill, and his mother had made a dish of potato salad and a pan of brownies. It was just enough to make the day complete. The four grandparents then stayed just long enough for Josh to open his gifts and to embrace Liz as if she were already a part of the family. They then excused themselves as they admitted it had been a grand and exciting event, but they were rather tired and needed to get home.

Later, when the others had settled down in front of the TV, Josh took Liz by the hand and walked to the pond where Tom and the boys had constructed a gazebo about three years ago. Liz was watching some ducks swimming in the pond and admiring the colorful flowers surrounding the gazebo, but Josh motioned for her to come and sit down. "Mom insisted on the padded bench," he explained by trying to imitate her when she'd said, "There's nothing worse, when you're trying to relax and enjoy a lovely evening outside, than having to sit on one of those hard wooden benches." Of course, he couldn't hold back a hearty laugh.

"It's such a beautiful setting, Josh, I could spend hours just enjoying the pond and its surroundings. I imagine it's much different from the way Christy saw it when she and Jon came last Christmas." She leaned back against his chest when he put his arms around her.

After a few minutes of just holding her, Josh reached down and took her left hand in his. As he massaged each finger and then started making circles on her palm, he said, "Liz, I have something very important to talk to you about. You know I've been captivated with you since the first day I saw you at the ranch although I really didn't treat you very well with my constant teasing. I've even tried to walk away so you could enjoy your high school years, but it seems apparent now that we are meant to be together. So, I'd like to show you tonight just how much I care for you." Quickly pulling a small box from his pocket, and with a big grin on his face, he'd turned so he was now facing her before he continued. "I want to give you this ring to wear from now through your high school graduation. Just think, you'll have a convenient date for all your school activities, and you won't need to be embarrassed having to ask one of those great big handsome hunks at school and maybe being turned down. I promise I'll never turn you down, Sweetheart."

"And after I'm out of school and don't need a convenient date anymore, will we then go our separate ways?" she asked quite solemnly.

"I hope you know better than that, Elizabeth Becker. Are you just trying to frustrate me when I'm trying to be very serious for a change? I'm expecting this engagement to end like most engagements do-- with a beautiful wedding ceremony."

"Oh," she gasped, "is this going to be an engagement ring? You said it was a ring for me to wear until I graduate." Grinning, she cupped his face in her hands, and with her lips so very close to his, she whispered, "I do love you, Josh."

He put his hand behind her head and drew her the following two inches so he could give her a soft quick kiss, but then gently he took her by the shoulders and pushed her a few inches away. "I love you, too, Princess, but I've got to finish this and I don't want any more interruptions from you. Will you please accept this **engagement ring** and promise to marry me on July 5, 2008? I promised your dad that I would make sure this is what you want, but you aren't helping, you know."

"You talked to my dad? I'll bet that was quite a conversation." She then giggled and asked, "Were you really talking to Dad about a wedding ceremony for you and me?"

"Not exactly the wedding ceremony, but I did talk to him about letting us be engaged for the next two years. He gave his consent only if it was what *you* wanted and not just for my satisfaction, so do you want me to continue?"

Liz watched as Josh struggled to keep his composure, but she suddenly became very serious and whispered, "I'm so sorry, Josh." She could hardly be heard, and her eyes were now filling with tears as her hands caressed his face. "I didn't mean to upset you. I don't know when it was that I realized I truly loved you because you were so exasperating at times. I certainly love getting back at you, when I can; but for you to want our wedding to be on the day I kissed you to wake you up from the coma is so sentimental. It means so much to me."

"What did you just say? Did you mean to tell me that, Liz, or did it just slip out?"

"Now, Josh, you're really not expecting to get two confessions on the same day, are you? You were the first boy, actually a 21 year old man, I'd ever kissed and I was scared to death. And to make it even worse was that Dr. Wilder had slipped into the room and heard me talking to you about whether I should actually kiss you or not."

Josh couldn't help laughing. "That's why he called you my fairy princess. You are so awesome, Sweetheart, and I don't know how you've kept that a secret for so long. But now, My Un-Mysterious Princess, do I get to put this engagement ring on your finger or do I have to get down on my knees and beg?"

"Oh, that would really be so sweet. Since this is most likely going to be my one and only marriage proposal, it should have all the exciting aspects, don't you think?"

"You're really going to pay for this, Elizabeth Becker," he grinned, "but I'm afraid you know that right now I'd do almost anything to get this ring on your finger." So, getting down on his knees, he opened the box for her to see the ring and then whispered,

"Please, Sweetheart, My Beautiful Mysterious Princess, and My Funny but Darling Liz, will you consent to be my wife in 2008 and let me put this ring on your finger as a token of my love?"

"Oh, wow!"

"Liz, that's not an answer. Don't you want to be engaged to me?" he moaned. "Your dad made me promise that I wouldn't force you into something you didn't want to do."

"Put that ring on my finger and then hold me tight before I faint. Oh, Josh, it's just so beautiful. I'll cherish it all my life, but not as much as I'll cherish you. Should we go inside and tell everybody? On second thought, maybe we'll do that later because I need a kiss right now and then I want to stay here in your arms, maybe forever."

"I'll love you forever, Princess, and I hope the next two years pass quickly so we can be married and live happily ever after." Josh breathed a sigh of relief when the ring was on her finger and their engagement had finally been sealed with a kiss. He'd returned to the bench and again pulled her back against his chest, and then he began to sing:

I'm just an old cowhand, from the Ranch so Grand,
And you're a little filly I would love to brand
With a ton of my kisses and a lot of love,

Wake with you in my arms and a blue sky above.
So-o-o, I'm gonna work hard the days and years ahead,
And I'll surely be ready for that day we're wed.
I can hardly wait to put on that wedding band
Because you're the little filly I'm gonna brand.
I'm just an old cowhand, from the Ranch so Grand.

"Oh, Josh, that was so sweet," she giggled. "You mentioned in an e-mail once that you'd like to sing to me, but that was going to be while we were riding. I think this was so much more romantic, and you do have a nice voice. I hope you'll sing to me often."

"I'll be happy to do that, Sweetheart."

Then, as Josh held Liz a little tighter and kissed the top of her head, he couldn't help but utter a prayer. "Dear God, the One who knows each of us so completely, our highs and our lows, our likes and our dislikes, the paths that we will follow and the mistakes we will undoubtedly make, I want to thank You for bringing Liz and me to the realization that this is your plan for us and you've always been walking beside us or leading the way even though we may have misread your guidelines at times. As I think of all the decisions we've made, whether right or wrong, you were always there guiding us to this night when our engagement makes the future look so extremely bright. Looking back, I can even be thankful for the fall from the horse because it helped bring me to this moment when I can promise to always be faithful to My Mysterious Princess. Amen."

"Amen," he heard her whisper.

Epilog

2 years later - - -

When into my crystal ball I peer,
It shows July 5, 2008 will soon be here.
A beautiful wedding is being planned, I see
At the ranch, of course, out under the maple tree.

I also see strangers who might appear
Just in time for this wedding here.
Maybe they're family, I cannot tell,
But they'll be here to wish them well.

A honeymoon will be meant for two
Who survived the years with a love so true.
Their happiness together is bound to be
Blessed with babies, one, two, or three.

Let us be thankful that God was there
To lead this young and daring pair.
They beat the odds that come with love
For they'd put their trust in our Lord above.

About the Author

Being one of the lucky ones, whose parents didn't have to move around after she was ready to start school, Sally went from first grade through graduation with the same group of friends, just adding more at the junior high and senior high shool levels. High school years can be filled not only with studies, but with dates, dances, sports events, stage productions, special clubs, and many other happy and rewarding times. There can also be some rather stressful decisions to be made about the future, but the years spent in high school are some of the most exciting of a person's life. Sally was only a teenager during WWII, but she got to know some of the servicemen who were stationed in Galesburg, Illinois, and corresponded with them after they'd been transferred. She also wrote to several during the Korean conflict which included her future husband. It was wonderful training in writing as she described in detail what was going on at home.

Sally found her first real love as a junior in High school. He was a year older and they had talked of marriage after she graduated, but that was not to be. However, now as she remembers her youth and romantic experiences, as well as watching her sons and grandchildren grow up, she has some insight for writing about the perplexing situations that Josh and Liz face in this touching story of young love.

Sally was retired and had moved to Lawrence, KS, before she actually decided to try writing a novel. She enjoys creating the characters, the events, and also the final conclusions.

CPSIA information can be obtained
at www.ICGtesting.com
Printed in the USA
FFOW02n1304150515
13462FF